For Karen

Wishing y...

birthday o...

Blessings,

Veronika

xxx

The Soapmaker

By Veronika Sophia Robinson

moonlight & motif

Magical Realism

The Soapmaker
© Veronika Sophia Robinson
© Cover art by Sarah Esau
ISBN 978-1-7393353-9-7
Published by Moonlight and Motif,
an imprint of Starflower Press
www.starflowerpress.com
Summer Solstice June 2023
Sun in Cancer, Moon in Leo, Jupiter in Taurus

British Library Cataloguing In Publication Data. A catalogue record for this book is available from the British Library.

Other novels by the same author
www.starflowerpress.com
www.veronikarobinson.com

Apple Wood, Bay & Rosemary Soap

There's a nebulous moment between when we're not here and when we are. It's like sunrise, as that crescent of fire hoists itself over the horizon. You can sense something changing, almost there, but not quite. Nearly there, nearly there, and then, suddenly, we're here.

At first, we're simply a collection of carefully chosen ingredients, each with our own stories, ushered around a vast stainless steel pot by her hand blender. And then, in that moment, we start to claim our wholeness. It's when she adds the final ingredients: herbs, flowers, roots, leaves; yes, that's when it happens: *the invocation*. She calls it magic. We call it A Knowing. All of a sudden, our place in this world is clear.

We start as one, here in the pot, and then we're divided as we're poured into wooden loaf tins; and once our beingness has firmed up, then we're divided again. Sliced into sections. We are bars of soap. She says we're not like ordinary supermarket soap manufactured in a factory. We're special. Crafted by her hands, and whispered into existence. Our purpose is ordained by her, our Maker. It's the same for all of us. We never know when it will be our turn, or to which mortal we'll be assigned. Most of the time, not even our Maker knows that. The only certainty we have is that once we start work, we don't have much time. Our mission is to imbue the human with hope, realisation and potentiality.

Our lives are brief.

The Soapmaking Studio

Apple wood for love. Grace grated the fresh twig across the metal grater, and scraped the pulp into the batch of soap ingredients. *Love,* she said out loud to ensure the oils heard and absorbed her intention. If she was going to surrender to love again, then this time it had to be right. No mistakes.

Grace learnt, long ago, at her grandmother's side, that apple wood is a sacred love charm and also used for prophesying. Upon blending the mixture, she poured it into ten large wooden moulds. Afterwards, an aromatic bay leaf and a sprinkle of rosemary needles were placed onto the batter-like liquid for decoration.

After washing her hands, Grace updated the blog on her website: dragonflysoaps.com

This morning in the studio I've been busy crafting a new soap that I'm so excited to share with you! If you're looking for love, be sure to add this to your collection. Apple wood, bay and rosemary will be ready for purchase in six weeks. Pre-orders available now.

This soap is a blend of almond and unrefined olive oils I've sourced from Fairtrade farms in Spain. To this, I've added organic coconut butter and local beeswax. To ensure it has a refreshing zing, I've infused it with pure essential oil of rosemary and bay. Although I don't make the oil myself, I do place rosemary leaves into the soap as it is setting.

This photo is of some of the thriving rosemary bushes in the garden. They smell heavenly!

Each of the botanicals has a job to do, whether it's to make soap hard or lather easily. Others make it creamy to the touch, nourishing to the senses, and conditioning to the skin.

Since ancient times, apple trees have been known as the Tree of Love. The addition of bay leaves in the soap boosts the magic.

Rosemary is for love, fidelity and wisdom. May love be yours! ~ Grace

By imbuing the mixture with a love spell for herself, she knew others would also benefit as soon as they held a bar of the soap in their hands. Satisfied that the spell was complete, she pushed the moulds to the far side of her wooden workbench. There, at the end, was a photo of her mother that she'd taken from her handbag earlier as a reminder to get it framed. The resemblance was such that people often thought her and Serena were twins: a smattering of lazy freckles sunbathing upon alabaster cheeks the colour of seashells, petite nose, a determined and spacious jawline, smokey-green eyes, and shoulder-length burnt-copper hair.

The past couple of years had been focused on her daughter, Lilac; alongside building up her soapmaking business far, far away from all she'd known. *There was no point being in the soap business if you couldn't clean your own life.* The move from Australia to Cumbria had been harrowing. At every step of the way, she faced challenges, choices and changes. With time, came healing. With healing, came possibilities. Today, however, Grace felt fragile and vulnerable against life's tides. It was nothing she could pinpoint, just a dip in how she was feeling. Staying strong every day was exhausting. This morning, between slumber and waking, Grace was certain that she'd heard her mother call out her name: *Rebecca*. "I'm Grace, now," she whispered. "Remember?"

Tracing the outline of her mother's face in the photo, it was as if she could almost still smell the air of her home town. Grace missed the charming coffee shops and the artisan boutiques and galleries brimming with local wares like silver jewellery and hand-thrown pottery. If only she could go back for one last chai latte at the Two Sisters Bakery. There she'd watch young mums stroll by with babies wrapped in colourful cotton slings. Friday mornings greeted her with the scent of sourdough rye. The bakery was in a beautiful wooden house, with a wrap-around verandah, just near the beach. As apple pies cooled atop wire racks on the window ledge, she'd sip her drink.

During the day, alongside her mother, she'd craft soaps in her seaside shop while chatting with tourists. Life had been perfect. In the space of one horrific hour, Byron Bay had changed. And so had she. Grace wondered if the blood would ever wash off her hands. Not even the Australian Seaweed and Wild Tasmanian Sloe sloughing soap seemed to cleanse the truth.

What she particularly missed now was walking through the scrubland and mountains, gathering items for soapmaking. In some bars of soap she'd place a single blossom from the dwarf-apple eucalyptus tree, symbolic of healing. On others, she'd add a gum nut when tying the soap with raffia. Each bar of soap had a piece of Australia embedded, such as sunshine-yellow wattle blossom.

Home.

An unguarded tear slipped away.

It pained Grace that Lilac could never learn the reason they'd moved so far away from all they'd loved, and lost. Her fingers wound around the pottery mug, inscribed with the words Two Sisters. It was one of only a handful of items, apart from clothing, that she'd brought with her from home. Although some items were kept in storage, she doubted there'd ever come a time when she'd ship them over. The past didn't deserve a place in her future.

Mornings were Grace's most productive time of day to work; she'd settle herself into the soap-making studio, with the conservatory doors flung wide open, and gather the ingredients for the day. A third-generation soapmaker, Grace carried on with certain aspects of the tradition while forsaking others, such as the use of tallow and lard. She chose, instead, to create plant-based soaps.

The studio was her favourite room to drink tea, and it gave her a calm space in which to gather her thoughts while preparing a list of the jobs for the day. Steam from the ginger tea twirled its way across the room. Reaching into an old pottery mug for a pen, she then wrote her to-do list.

The loaves she poured last night were setting nicely, she noticed later, as she checked through each of the wooden curing racks, brushing off soap flakes and tidying as she went. It excited her to see the wide range of colours as she arrived in her studio each day. Racks of vibrant hues, all created from plants, were visually luxurious and smelt heavenly: a sensuous blend that was all at once intoxicating, exotic, spicy, floral and calming.

Through the open doors, the familiar knocking sound of the garden's resident woodpecker made her smile. Positioned high in the cedar tree, he tap, tap, tapped. *Ah, you're back! Opportunity knocks.*

Dozens of geraniums in terracotta pots, lining the low windowsill, were now in full bloom. Their blasts of red blossoms peered out from the wiry lengths of scented green-leaved branches. Each flower competed for light as its colour punctuated the conservatory.

Without warning, the unbridled sunshine which had filtered in through the windows and glass roof all morning was eclipsed by sombre clouds. Grace shivered. Something in the air had shifted. "You're safe," she whispered, looking around the room in case she'd missed something. Or someone. "You're safe."

It took her a minute or two to regain her calm, then she placed thirty-six bars of freshly cut lemongrass and ginger soap onto the rack. Next up were the dandelion and cardamom bars of soap. Standing back to survey the studio, Grace sighed with delight as she breathed in the exquisite scents.

The racks were quite full already, and she knew that at some point soon, with business expanding so rapidly, she'd need to get some more built. Frustrated that the man who'd built these racks had retired, she'd left a note on her fridge this morning: Find a carpenter! For weeks she'd been telling herself to look online at reviews of local tradesmen, but each day she'd get so sidetracked in the studio that it simply escaped her thoughts. Next on her list was developing the cornflower and thyme soap recipe. She needed to add alkanet root to change the hue. Today she was also preparing two other new recipes: Apple mint and lime flower; and chai tea with sweet orange and clove.

It had been more than a year and a half now since she moved to Dragonfly Cottage. A full year of seasons and sighs, of hope and bone-aching homesickness. This year would be different, and she knew it. Change was in the air, and she could feel it as solidly as the soap bar in her hands.

Grace cleared the bench space to prepare for the task ahead: labelling the chamomile-and-yarrow soap bars which had now fully cured. She was so pleased at the first year's harvest of herbs and flowers from her garden. After wrapping a bar of soap in a strip of textured cream-coloured card, she ran her fingers over the words on the label:

Chamomile and Yarrow Soap
For peace, calm, abundance,
healing and protection
Artisan & 100% Botanical
Handcrafted with love

Dragonfly Cottage Soaps

When she moved in, Grace deliberately changed the name of her house from Lane End Farm to Dragonfly Cottage. After that fateful day, the trauma counsellor had said it might be helpful to find a totem animal to act as an anchor through her transformation. She'd scoffed at the ludicrous idea. "How the hell is a totem animal going to undo all this?" But now, here in her self-created sanctuary, she acknowledged how helpful it had been on her healing path.

Byron Bay, Australia

"Mummy, look at the dragonfly's pretty green and purple wings!" Lilac exclaimed that Sunday afternoon as they strolled hand in hand, and plucked flowers from the sedges. It was their final week in Australia and Grace wanted to breathe in every last bit of her homeland. "She looks like she's hiding, doesn't she?" The little girl bent in closely to examine the insect.

Hiding.

"Yes, she does, sweetheart."

"Maybe she has a secret, Mummy?" Lilac whispered.

That night, when Lilac drifted off to sleep, Grace flipped open her book on insects of Australia, and made notes:

The favoured place for female dragonflies to forage is in flower meadows. As they are secretive, it's only when they're ready to mate that they'll come near water.

At her final counselling session in Australia, the therapist gifted her a mug illustrated with dragonflies.

"I can't believe you've given me this mug. It's too coincidental!" Grace welled up. "I wanted to talk to you today about dragonflies. I wondered if it might be my totem animal."

Grace voraciously researched dragonflies for days afterwards. If it were true that they were symbolic of hope, change, love, happiness and new beginnings, then she would ensure her life was wrapped in every inch of the totem's symbolism.

Once Grace had finished labelling the soaps, and packed them for shipping to her stockists, she picked up the full bucket and went to empty yesterday's compost. A favourite chore, it gave her a chance to walk down to the end of the garden and take in some fresh air. Without putting on shoes, she stepped upon the moss-filled lawn, so soft underfoot and damp from last night's rain, and listened to the blackbird call. As she tipped the contents of lavender stems, eucalyptus twigs, orange rind, bits of clay, and scrapings of coconut butter into the compost area, Grace thought she saw movement out of the corner of her eye.

In a moment of panic, she dropped the empty bucket. "Damn it!" It bothered her that she always felt so out of control; she never used to be like this. Living up a private, one-way country road made her alert to any unexpected visitors. Ever hypervigilant, she could usually hear a car long before she saw it, but these people were on foot, which took her completely by surprise. The rush of fear quickly dissipated as soon as she noted their clothing and accessories: business suit and briefcase. Immediately she knew that her morning was about to be interrupted by Jehovah's Witnesses. Over the years she'd had many knocks on her door, but this was the first time any of them called at Dragonfly Cottage. *I guess they're the same as in Australia.* As much as she felt it was a violation of privacy and one's belief system to have random strangers banging on the door espousing their religion, she just wasn't of the disposition to chase them away. It just wasn't in her nature to be mean.

As the couple came within a few metres of her garden gate, Grace called out "Good morning, coming to convert me then?" She laughed it off, but was quite surprised by the twist in her belly when the man smiled. All she could think was: *why is someone as handsome as you a Bible basher?*

Having once befriended a Jehovah's Witness at school, she knew members weren't keen on hearing about other people's ideas. Grace was also wise enough to know that when someone had been brainwashed into it that there was nothing you could say to convince them otherwise.

"Good morning," he smiled, raising his hand to the sunshine which had returned. "Lovely day, isn't it?"

What the hell was that? If Grace didn't know any better, she'd have guessed that he felt it too: with a single smile something incendiary had ignited between them.

"We've come to share the Watchtower magazine and tell you about the New World that's coming."

"Better come in then!" Grace smiled, beckoning them both indoors. They followed her into the kitchen.

"I'm Grace."

"I'm Caleb, and this is Madge."

"May I offer you a drink? I've just pressed some fresh apple juice this morning," Grace said, inviting them to sit at the kitchen table.

"Sounds lovely," he said. "Thank you."

Grace wondered if the woman was mute, and then remembered from her previous encounters that Jehovah's Witness women often appeared subservient in the company of men.

Madge nodded, and said "Yes please."

"Just give me a minute to wash my hands. I've been putting out the compost," Grace said, placing the bucket by the sink.

Madge spoke up. "Compost?"

"Yes, don't you compost? You know, put your plant scraps like vegetable and fruit peelings into a container to rot down for reuse later on?"

"Oh, I know what it is," Madge said. "It's just that you don't need to compost or recycle. In the New World, Jehovah will make everything perfect again."

Although Grace wasn't a violent person, there was something about Madge that sure made her want to slap the woman. *How ignorant could a person be?*

"So, you're saying we can trash the Earth and it doesn't matter?" Grace asked, her jaw tightening, as she placed the tumblers of juice on the table.

"Jehovah will make it right." Madge was adamant.

Astonished, Grace looked at Caleb to see if he agreed with the rubbish coming out of the woman's mouth. She noticed he was engrossed in reading a poster on her fridge for the local Extinction Rebellion rally.

"Do you agree with this, Caleb?" Grace asked.

He turned, startled, and then surprised her by knowing what they'd been discussing.

"I do compost, but according to our teachings, Jehovah will make the world new again and restore Paradise to Earth."

"Well, why do you compost then?" she asked.

Madge turned to look his way then interrupted before he could reply. "He just likes gardening, that's all. I always tell him not to bother putting it out, but he's in the habit."

"You're married? To each other?" Grace hadn't meant it to come out that way, but nothing about them matched. Their energy was totally out of alignment.

"Yes," Madge replied. "Since I was eighteen."

Madge continued to chat, far too much now for Grace's liking, so she interrupted.

"Waiting for the New World is all well and good, Madge, but quite frankly, it's a cop out and utterly irresponsible."

Frustration fuelled her now, and she noticed that Madge had reached down for her handbag readying herself to leave. Grace continued: "It's selfish not to take care of the Earth, regardless of your religion. We all share this planet," she said, exasperated. "All of us! No one has the right to destroy or poison it!"

"All these things that worry you really don't matter," Madge said as she pointed to the poster on the fridge. "You could save yourself a lot of time by not going on protest marches. Jehovah will return the Earth to paradise. He promised us. Thank you for your time," Madge said. "I hope you'll read The Watchtower magazine. You'll see things differently." She left her juice, still full in the glass, abandoned on the table. Madge headed up the hallway, and out the front door, without looking back, and was walking up the white-pebbled garden path within seconds.

When Caleb reached out to shake Grace's hand, she studied his eyes. *Blue, like cornflower soap. Kind, like gentle Spring rain. I could just rest here forever.* Why did he feel so safe? Everything she'd ever learnt about energy awareness was calling out to her and it was as if she felt something wasn't right for him. As if, somehow, he was out of place.

"Nice to meet you, Caleb." What Grace wanted to say was "I hope we meet again", but that was utterly ridiculous. The last thing she needed in her life was some nutcase preaching about an imaginary

New World. Or married! She knew one thing, though: she *did* want to see him again. The magnetic pull was overpowering.

"Have a lovely day, Grace. Thank you for your time." When he shook her hand for longer than she'd have expected from a stranger, Grace knew that she was in trouble. She didn't want him to let go. With Madge now well out of view, Grace wished she could stop time. She didn't want him to leave the kitchen. Reluctantly letting go of her hand, Caleb gave her one last half smile, then left.

Grace stood at her front door, and as she watched them walk up the road for some way, she noticed Madge didn't wait for Caleb.

Married? Grace shook her head, and walked back to the studio. *No. They just don't match!*

The Man in the Mirror

Caleb adjusted his blue tie, barely recognising his reflection in the mirror. *Who am I? What's the truth, and what isn't?*

"Hurry up, Caleb. We need to leave now!" Madge called from downstairs. "I don't want to be late like we were last week. What always takes you so long?"

The undisguised terseness in her voice unsettled him. For years, he'd accommodated her ability to irritate or offend everyone around her; often cleaning up Madge's mess by apologising on her behalf.

Thursday evenings at 6.40pm were always the same: Caleb dragging his feet to avoid getting dressed in his suit; stalling at the constrictive tie, symbolic of his life in a noose; Madge itching to get out the door to worship at the Kingdom Hall in Carlisle.

When did he change his mind? At what point did the teachings he'd known all his life stop making sense? Grappling with these burning questions, and no one to discuss them with, Caleb tried in vain to bury them. He wondered now, for a half a moment, if he just shouldn't feign sickness this evening. Let her go off without him. As he took one last glance in the mirror, a thought occurred to him. *I wonder what Grace is doing tonight?*

"Caleb! Now!"

Calmly walking down the stairs, he heard Madge say "I'm going to visit Suzi afterwards."

Their seventeen-year-old daughter, Ciara, looked up from her mobile phone. "Arthur's coming here after the meeting. I need you to chaperone, Dad."

Caleb could barely contain his sigh.

"Dad!"

"Yes, fine."

"You know we can't be alone. It's your spiritual responsibility as my father to chaperone us during our courtship! Why are you making a fuss about it?"

"I didn't make a fuss, Ciara. Maybe I just wanted a few moments this evening to myself. Is that too much to ask?"

"Yes!" she snapped, head hunched forward over the phone.

"Hurry up you two!" Madge said, walking out the door and pointedly jangling the car keys in Caleb's direction.

What happened to my little family? When did we change?

They drove in silence to the Kingdom Hall, Caleb's thoughts never too far from Grace's pretty cottage. As they waited at red lights, he thought about her farmhouse kitchen, and the signs of life: of happiness, and of freedom. Her home was simply decorated but it was obvious that each item had been chosen with great care and love; nothing unnecessary or unwanted.

Caleb switched on the car radio to rid himself of Grace; he knew it was wrong to imagine spending time with her.

"Tonight we're talking about the recent spate of sheep deaths in south Cumbria, the environment, and Summer gardening tips," came the announcer's voice.

"Oh no, Mum's still feeling poorly after her chemo," Madge said, looking up from the text she was reading, and then wiped the tear trickling down her cheek.

"I'm sorry to hear that. Give her my love," Caleb said. "Can we do anything for her?"

"I'll go and visit her tomorrow," Madge replied. "I hate that she lives so far away. I think she should come and live with us."

"In a two-bedroom house?" he choked, nearly driving off the road.

"Why not? She could share the master bedroom with me, and you could sleep on the sofa," Madge said, as if it was the most obvious solution.

"Of course. Whatever she needs."

Neither of them had heard the report on sheep deaths, but when the announcer said "The environment is in poor shape," Caleb turned the volume up. "On a daily basis mankind is causing irreparable damage. Welcome to BBC Cumbria if you're just tuning in."

Madge switched off the radio. "We don't need to hear that."

"I'm listening," Caleb said, his voice calm, as he turned it back on.

"Tonight we have the organiser of the local Extinction Rebellion group with us to talk about their next planned rally in Carlisle City Centre. Grace Lysander, welcome to the show."

"Thank you, Max," she said, her voice warm and gentle.

"Grace, why is the cause so close to your heart?"

Recognising the soft Australian accent, Madge immediately looked over at Caleb. "Did you know she'd be on the radio?"

"What are you talking about? How could I know that?" Caleb shook his head in disbelief.

Madge turned off the radio once more, and changed the subject.

"Why didn't you shave?" Madge demanded as they pulled into the parking lot at the Kingdom Hall. "You're an elder. You should be setting an example! You know the other elders will counsel you about it."

Caleb shrugged; he simply didn't care. It wasn't anyone's business what he did with his body.

Ciara had been quiet in the back seat for the duration of the journey. She looked up from her phone. "Why are you two bickering? It's awful!"

"You need to get involved, Caleb," Madge continued. "Be more active in Bible study. Focus on Jehovah," she said, getting out and slamming the car door.

The Macadamia Nut Grove
New South Wales, Australia

Rebecca could never remember if her first memory was watching her Grandpa as he cold pressed the macadamia nuts or her Grandma churning soap with the oil he'd made from them. What she did learn early on was that the oil wasn't prone to rancidity, and that it provided a reliable conditioning lather in soapmaking. Grandpa would boast that the light, golden-coloured oil, which came from the pressed nuts, was so nourishing for the skin because it was rich in Vitamins A, B1, B2, E and K. He said it was excellent for treating sunburn, wounds and scars because it was so highly absorbable. Rebecca took in all these facts by osmosis like other toddlers learnt colours or numbers.

From before she could walk, one or other of them would raise her up on their workbench and say "This will all be yours one day". It was only natural that she'd end up becoming both a soaper, like her grandmother and mother, but also the successful owner of a thriving macadamia nut grove. Reluctant to give up either, she chose to bring in a manager for the grove while she focused on soapmaking with Serena.

As an only child, she learnt to make her own fun under the canopy of the 'mac trees', as she called them. They offered magical shadows on days when the clouds hung low, and glorious streams of light between leaves when the Sun was beaming bright. Beneath the leafy skyscape overhead, she crafted soaps in disused moulds, filling them with mud, adorning each mould with macadamia blossoms, leaves and nuts; demonstrating creative flair from an early age.

The beautiful wooden homestead, nestled in the nut grove, had been built in the 1930s, and was just 25 minutes from Byron Bay. Serena also lived on the property, about half a mile away. Located near hills, covered in tranquil subtropical rainforests, it was a botanical paradise for soapmaking.

As Rebecca sat on the verandah that afternoon with her best friend, Angie, reading through the Real Estate listing, it seemed incomprehensible that the only life she'd ever known was all coming to an end.

"This is where I gave birth to Lilac, and watched her learn to walk on the lawn. This is our home. This is my place on Mother Earth, my patch of paradise."

Angie held her hand. "Are you sure selling it is the right thing to do? Maybe you could move to the other side of Oz under the Witness Protection offer, and rent this place out?"

"I know. I just feel the only way I can be certain Lilac is safe is by going far away. If I do Witness Protection, I can never contact friends again. That's just a step too far."

"I'm sure going to miss you. We've known each other since kindy. God knows how I'll live without you, mate. Have you chosen your new name yet?"

"Yeah."

"And?"

"Grace Lysander."

"Why have you chosen that?"

"All I've thought about since that day is 'there but for the grace of God'; I'm always wondering why I was saved."

"And the surname?"

"Lysander means liberation. Freedom. And I could sure do with being free of this inner hell."

"I hope you find it, honey. I really do." Angie took the Real Estate brochure from Rebecca's hands to read.

Paradise For Sale

Over three generations, these 65 acres with stunning views of the Nightcap Mountain Ranges have grown to provide an established income from the 3,000 mature macadamia-nut trees.

Even in times of drought, this business has thrived due to the spring-fed extensive irrigation system.

The property features two homesteads and three industrial, powered sheds. Diversification by the current owner has included five fully-furnished glamping yurts with communal kitchens, private amenities, and BBQ areas.

This unique and stunning venue, set in the rolling hills of fertile and lush hinterland, is a featured wedding-ceremony venue by Bride magazine.

Rebecca flicked open her phone and viewed photos of the property in Cumbria that she had put in an offer for, and tried to imagine what life would be like in a temperate climate.

"It looks so you!" Angie said, leaning in closely, and admiring the old English farmhouse with expansive oak-beamed conservatory and rambling gardens, apple orchard, meadows and views of the fells.

Rebecca wondered if she'd make new friends. And could she give Lilac the wonderful life they had here on their Australian property? There were so many unanswered questions.

"Well, Grace, if anyone can do this, you can. You've always been strong, capable, optimistic and determined. I've no doubt you'll create an amazing life."

"Grace," Rebecca repeated after her, listening to the sound of her new name. And again, she said it, more slowly this time. "Grace. Do you think it suits me?"

"Absolutely!"

Lullabies and Dragonflies

"Mummy, tell me the dragonfly story again." Lilac's request came each evening just after Grace had finished singing her the Australian hug lullaby. It was the same one Serena sang to her in childhood. Grace never knew if it was Lilac's way of deferring sleep or if she really did want the story.

"Mummy, please?" Lilac asked, eyes open wide in the way which always made Grace give in.

"Once upon a time, there lived a beautiful dragonfly named Asali. Her wings were luminous pink, green and purple, and they shimmered in the sunlight. Asali scurried across the water, flying to sedges and over the meadow and then back to the water. No matter where she went, she was always happy and her heart was full. Sometimes, she'd catch a glimpse of her face in the water. Even though she was elegant and graceful, Asali knew that no matter what she looked like, true beauty came from being kind. Wherever she flew, Asali brought hope, change, happiness, new beginnings and love."

Grace kissed Lilac's forehead, grateful for how quickly she succumbed to the sweet call of sleep. Inching herself off the bed, ever so slowly so as not to risk waking her daughter, she crept away.

In the kitchen, she flicked on the kettle and then opened her laptop.

Do Jehovah's Witnesses practise environmental care?

When she typed her question into the search engine, she was surprised to see how many results showed up. Grace hit the first link.

Finding herself in an ex-JW forum, she read through one of the comments in reply to a question about protecting the Earth.

There's no promotion of recycling or ways to conserve the environment. Everything is just left to Jehovah! They shamelessly pollute the landscape.

One time an elder lectured me long and hard about why it was pointless to belong to any conservation groups. He said that Jehovah would solve all the issues we had and that it was spiritually dangerous to be a member of any conservation group as they are political activists.

Witnesses are just doing whatever they want to the Earth. It scares me. This is everyone's planet and we all need to play a part.

After fixing herself a pot of chamomile tea, Grace moved on to another link, and laughed at the difference between her and Madge. It stated that a Jehovah's Witness proclaiming the end of the world is considered a crank, and a non-religious person saying the world is ending is an eco-warrior. It was true that Grace's passion for protecting the environment and walking lightly upon the Earth was at the forefront of many lifestyle choices.

She reflected on the article's likening of climate-change alarmism to religious apocalypticism. Lifting the tea bag out of the pot and onto a saucer, Grace pondered her own narrative of climate change. What started as a search on Jehovah's Witnesses soon had her scribbling down a reminder:

Email the school mums about the Extinction Rebellion rally.

Tell them where to meet, what to do, and what to bring for the march.

The Cabinet Maker

Lilac ran into the soapmaking studio to find Grace. "Mummy, Mummy! Look! This envelope came through the letterbox but it wasn't from the postman."

Lilac passed the cream-coloured envelope to her mother.

"Thanks honey," Grace said. "Are you ready for school yet?"

"Yes!"

"Great. Grab your lunch from the kitchen bench while I read this."

Dressed in faded denim jeans and a sage-green t-shirt, Grace tied up her shoulder-length hair into a high ponytail, and finished scribbling down her thoughts for a new soap recipe she was divining.

Ginseng for adaptability
Black pepper to symbolise what is missing from life
Lime for fidelity

Grace opened the envelope and began reading.

Dear Grace, I noticed the note on your fridge: 'find a carpenter'. I enclose my business card. Call if I can be of service. Regards, Caleb

Caleb Alden
Cabinet Maker and Carpenter
07171 444 978

A cabinet maker and carpenter? Perfect! But, a hot

carpenter in my workspace is going to drive me wild! She smiled, and then headed to the kitchen to meet Lilac.

"Right, sweetie, let's go."

They walked hand in hand that morning as Lilac looked out for wildflowers alongside the hedgerow.

"That's the cuckooflower, isn't it, Mummy?" Lilac said as she pointed to its delicate pale pink blossoms.

Grateful for the days when the weather held out long enough that they could walk the half mile to the village school, Grace squeezed Lilac's hand that bit tighter. "That's right, honey. It usually starts to bloom when the first cuckoo call of the year is heard. It likes to grow in moist soil, and that's why it's on this side of the hedgerow where it's shady."

Ten minutes later, Lilac asked "How did we get to school so quickly?"

"I don't know. It must be all that flower spotting. Give me a big hug."

Breathing in the scent of chamomile soap on her daughter's skin, a reminder of their English country garden, she kissed Lilac's cheeks.

"Keep being wonderful! See you this afternoon."

"Bye Mummy!"

She watched as Lilac skipped across the small school playground. It was divided up into child-sized vegetable, herb and flower beds, a living-willow dome, and wooden play area complete with horse-sized unicorn.

Grace returned home eager to phone Caleb. Each time she started typing in his number, she stopped about half way. It was true that she desperately needed a carpenter, but she couldn't ignore the seismic reaction between them. If there was anything she'd promised herself, it was this: don't court danger. Torn between listening to the encouraging voice within and the experiences of her past, Grace dialled his number in full. Her heartbeat drummed louder than the ring tone on her phone. *What if he answers?* She panicked. *What if he doesn't answer?* She no longer knew which was worse.

"Caleb Alden. May I help you?"

"It's…" Speech paralysis overwhelmed her.

"Hello?"

Silence.

Grace wanted to say in her most friendly voice, "Hi, it's Grace," but nothing came.

"Is anyone there? Can I help you at all?"

"I'm… It's Grace. You dropped off your card. Your business card."

"Hello Grace. Are you okay?"

"Yes, sorry."

"You're looking for a carpenter? What do you need?"

Her face, now tomato red, had flushed with embarrassment.

"Can we meet?" she asked, regretting it the second she spoke. It all sounded so wrong. "What I mean is that it might be easier to show you what I need." And still, with each word she felt more like a teenage girl rather than a competent business woman.

"That's no problem. I've actually got a few hours spare today. Would it suit you if I came by now?"

That was not what she was expecting.

"Um…"

"It's fine. If you want to schedule an appointment for another day, I'll grab my diary," he offered, accommodating her obvious hesitation.

"No, Caleb, come now. Today's good. You know

where I live. Instead of coming to the front door, go to the right and walk around the side past the honeysuckle and you'll see a conservatory. I'm here, in my studio. You can't miss it."

"See you in twenty to twenty-five minutes then," he said.

"Right. Bye." Grace raced to the mirror. Although she'd felt herself flush, to see the reality of it was worse. "Oh my God!" Placing her hands against each cheek with the intent of cooling them, Grace stepped outside hoping the fresh air might help. "He's a carpenter. That's all. He's just coming to take measurements. He's married. Stop it. Stop it! You need a job done, and he's the man for it. Nothing more. Stop it, Grace!"

Back inside the studio, she studied the curing racks, swiping away flakes of soap, ensuring everything was just so. Nothing out of place.

Twenty minutes felt like two. And there he was: standing at the doorway.

Grace looked up, caught off guard by his warm smile. She thought he was good looking in his suit but seeing him in denim jeans and t-shirt, with a leather work belt around his hips, made her swoon. How the hell would she get any work done if he was in the studio day after day?

"It sure smells pretty in here. What is that scent?" he asked, looking curiously around the studio. "So," he said, when she didn't reply. "What do you need doing?"

"Well, quite a few things," embarrassed by her sudden tongue-tie. "I need more curing racks."

"Curing?"

"Yes, what you can smell is the scent of the soaps I make. I need racks to put the soap on so that they can cure; to dry out. I also need some more wooden moulds made," she said, grabbing one from the bench and passing it to him.

Thankful that their hands didn't touch, she walked over to her three curing racks. "I could do with about ten more. I've got space over there against that wall. And I wouldn't mind a few more wooden paddles for stirring the mixes. Do you think this is the sort of thing you can do?"

"Well, I've never been in a soapmaking studio before but these are definitely all things I can make. When would you like me to start?"

"You'll do it, then?"

"Yes, if you'd like me to."

"That's fabulous. Thank you! You can start whenever you like. I only work school hours so I can be here when Lilac's at home. I sometimes work at night when she's in bed, but mostly I try to just work by day."

"Lilac? Your daughter? The little girl whose photos are all over your fridge?" he smiled. "She looks like you. Pretty. Only shorter!"

Grace was surprised by how relaxed she suddenly felt. "Well, she definitely got the maternal genes." She wanted to say 'thankfully' but thought better of it.

"You're on your own then?"

"No. I have Lilac."

"I meant…"

"I know what you meant. I'm not alone."

"I've got a couple of urgent jobs I need to finish which I can get done this afternoon. Shall I start tomorrow, say about 9?"

"Let's make it 9.30. It'll give me a chance to get back from the school run."

"See you then," he said, stepping backwards out of the door.

"Caleb," she said impulsively, stepping closer. "Would you like some soap?"

"Soap?"

Amused, she asked "You do take baths and showers, don't you?"

"Yes, I do," he smiled. "You don't think they're a bit feminine for me?"

"I do make soaps for men, you know! Wait there!"

Grace opened one of her pine cupboards. Scouring the fifteen varieties of soap she'd blended specifically for men, she knew immediately what Caleb needed. She retrieved a small bar of soap: Seaweed, Spiced Orange and Cedar.

"This should be perfect," Grace said, passing him the small soap.

Caleb breathed in the scent. "Grace, that's exquisite. How do you do that? I don't think I've ever smelled a soap that was so perfect before. This is really kind. Thank you so much. This might sound odd, but... No, never mind."

"What is it? What were you going to say?"

"It feels like it was made just for me."

"I made it before we met. Lucky coincidence, I guess. Oh," she said, suddenly remembering. "Madge! Your wife," Grace said, looking at him directly without blinking. "I'll find something for her. Just a minute."

"No, it's fine. You've been more than generous. Honestly."

"It's really no problem!" she said, heading to one of her other cupboards.

"Grace, I'd rather you didn't," he said firmly.

His tone stopped Grace in her tracks. "Fine. No

worries," she said, trying to dismiss the kick in the gut she suddenly felt.

"See you in the morning. Thank you," he said again, his tone softening. "This really is so kind."

She smiled, but inside something was amiss. Had she read him wrongly? Why did she suddenly feel so uncomfortable? It was as if she'd crossed a boundary and undone their easy rapport. Conflict made her feel uncomfortable. It wasn't as if he was cross, but he had been firm. Bringing Madge into the equation was clearly not an option.

Grace watched him walk across the garden and out of view. *Disentangle yourself*, she said, hoping the words would catch up and settle in his heart. If nothing else, the soap would work. She was sure of that. It always did.

Memories of The Gathering

High Spring Tide, a year before

Lilac frolicked along the shoreline, salt air in her vivid-red hair with gold undertones. Several steps ahead of Grace, she gathered items of interest on their first beachcombing adventure in Cumbria. They'd not walked along a beach since they'd lived in Australia. They wandered now, along wide expansive sands of Beckfoot Beach, the repetitive lull of the incoming waves a soundtrack to the open views of the Solway Firth.

The sugar kelp willingly offered itself up in abundance to the sandy shore. The high Spring tides brought with it the expected gifts of spiral-turned shells, opaque sea glass, weathered driftwood; and the unwanted filthy refuse from mankind's exploitations: an oil drum, rubber tyre, and plastic bags strewn as far as Grace could see. It troubled her, this discord between the beauty of the natural world and the sordid reminder of anonymous thoughtlessness. Gathering handfuls of the seaweed, with the intention of adding it to her soapmaking repertoire, she placed the fronds in a basket; and stuffed bits of rubbish brought up from the storm into an old bag.

"Lilac, honey, come and look at this," she called, beckoning her close.

"What is it, Mummy?" Lilac asked, looking up from a rock pool where she was examining a small crab skeleton.

"This sugar kelp."

"It's everywhere, isn't it?" Lilac exclaimed, skipping along the sand with all the freedom of a child protected from the realities of adult life.

"In the olden days," Grace said, holding a piece in the air, "people who lived by the sea would hang fronds like this up to dry. If it stayed dry, the weather would be fine. But if it became soft and limp, rain was on the way."

"Can we take some and try it, Mummy?"

"Sure we can. They used to call it the poor man's weather glass."

"What do you think it will do? Will it dry out?"

"We'll just have to wait and see. Maybe we can tie some to the apple tree. In the meantime, I also have this basketful of kelp to use in some soap."

Last Christmas

Christmas spices lingered lazily around the old farmhouse kitchen that snowy Winter's morning. Silently, the outdoor landscape saluted the layer upon layer of slow-falling snowflakes assembling in the garden and out across the open meadows.

The secluded cottage was comfortably cocooned from the crazy commercialism being conducted in Carlisle city centre and small-town Penrith.

Lilac punctuated the rolled-out-dough mix with her silver star-shaped cutter.

"Rudolph", she sang, swinging her hips side to side in time with the jazzy New Orleans rendition of her favourite song. "Rudolph!"

On the other side of the wooden kitchen table, Grace dipped the slices of orange into the spice mix of cinnamon, nutmeg and cloves, then placed them into the dehydrator to dry. Satisfied that she'd made a colourful collection of scented decorations for the Christmas tree, she then sliced and spiced another dozen oranges for a soap recipe she had in mind.

Forest hike, Australia, ten years prior

Rebecca and her grandma, Anna, hiked up the path of the Nightcap Mountain Range. This was their annual gathering of the first fresh needles of cedar in the springtime. The forest air was cool, but this was the best time to harvest for soapmaking. Little did Rebecca know that in years from now she'd be gathering cedar from Scotland. Before Rebecca had even learnt to walk, Anna would carry her up the mountain in a sling, imbuing her with the feel of the land, and how to use plants in soapmaking.

.

Seaweed, Spiced Orange & Cedar Soap

We first became aware of ourselves, as soap, one morning when her voice came soft and slow, almost like she was singing. We listened intently while she told us things that were important to remember. They were the reason she made us, she'd said. At first, she blended the batter with an electric mixer. And then, with a wooden paddle in her hand, she stirred us, her final ingredients, around and around, slowly adding more to our tribe.

Handfuls of finely chopped seaweed were folded into our being as if she were feeding us, filling us up. We adapted to this foreign invader until we knew no separation.

"Seaweed" Grace said, "for looking below the surface. Help them to tap into unseen gifts." It was then that we were told the reason for our existence. "To disentangle," she said. "It's time to let go of anything or anyone that doesn't serve you."

Seaweed was bursting with stories of her adventures, and recounted how she'd spent a lifetime dancing in the ocean moving with the tides, free and flexible, this way and that.

Swimming.

Swaying.

Swinging.

Hers was a life of freedom, untethered to anything. Seaweed told us she'd been gathered from the Cumbrian coastline, and collected in the bare hands of our Maker. Seaweed's calmness ensured that, no matter what happened, everything would be okay.

We were soon joined by another visitor. Our

Maker snipped small triangular pieces of dried spiced orange alongside us. Spiced Orange delighted us with her excitement. Oh, the stories she told! There were fun and festivities witnessed in the kitchen last Christmas, and she spoke of an early life on a Spanish orange grove where her days were lived out in glorious sunshine. She spun around us, her spices leaving sparkling specks in our space as she spread her happy spirit. With each turn of the wooden paddle, our Maker whispered words in time with the spiral movements.

"Spiced orange for energy, good cheer, excitement and adventure."

When Cedar joined us, we were regaled with his tales of mountain life and the wisdom he'd gleaned from his ancestors. We listened intently, fascinated by how we'd work together.

With one final stir of the paddle, we heard the words: *Cedar for strength and spiritual connection.*

Steam and Spice

As Caleb waited for the shower to warm up, he suddenly remembered the soap. Peering out of the bathroom to check Madge wasn't still getting dressed in their bedroom, he quickly stepped over to his bedside drawer. Feeling like a thief in the night, he reached beneath his neatly folded underwear and took out the bar of the soap. The scent was intoxicating.

It was the first time in their marriage that he'd ever locked the bathroom door. The guilt rose like sewage gurgling up gutter drains in a storm. *It's just a bar of soap. Why does it feel so sinful?*

In less than an hour he'd be at Grace's home working on the jobs she needed doing around the studio. Truth was, he couldn't remember the last time he felt so excited about going to work. Carpentry hadn't been his first job choice, but he'd been content enough. Over time he developed his skills and became a cabinet maker. Caleb's childhood dream, however, was to be a rural vet with his own practice. As he inched closer to leaving school, the elders at the Kingdom Hall had warned him from attending university. "We don't recommend you go. It's too worldly. There are too many influences, Caleb. And besides, in the New World there won't be a need for veterinary science. Why don't you become a window cleaner, Caleb? That's what all the other young lads do. Then you'll have plenty of time to go on the ministry. Jehovah's work is important. We need more people like you knocking on doors and sharing The Watchtower magazine with people." Caleb could hear the words just as clearly, all these years later. Although he'd started off window cleaning, he quickly decided that he preferred working with wood.

Deliberately not turning on the extractor fan in the bathroom, Caleb breathed in the thick steam now heavily scented with spiced orange and cedar. Watching the bathroom clock, he counted down the minutes until he'd see Grace. Like a man possessed, he admonished himself. *You're a married man! You're a servant of Jehovah! What are you thinking?*

Distracting himself by counting the tiles, he remembered the week he spent decorating the bathroom. Tile after tile, scraping on grout, and creating a home for the three of them. Although home ownership isn't encouraged by the Witness community, Caleb had a deep yearning to create a place which felt like theirs even though it was rented. So, each night after he'd finished work, he transformed the bathroom so that it was a place of calm in their home. Tile after tile, he counted, until he reached the last one. Eighty seven.

As he held the soap, it was as if Grace was in the shower with him. Closing his eyes, Caleb dared to imagine. With each movement of the soap against his skin, he washed away his cares. *What is in this soap?* A shower had never felt so enlivening. At first he washed his chest, strong from years of using a hand-held saw to cut wood; then around his solid, tanned neck and over his taut shoulders muscles, then under his arms.

The steam should have helped him to breathe more easily, but with each heightened thought of Grace he found himself in rapture and blissful joy. It was as if, for the first time in his life, he was standing at the doorway of his cage and the door was open. Hope surged through his veins.

Washing between his legs, he softly said "Down Shep". Impossible to defeat an arousal, he succumbed to the intense pleasure coursing through his body when he was startled out of his reverie by the sound of tugging on the door handle. The soap dropped to the bottom of the shower just as Madge called out "Why have you locked the door?"

"Did I?" he asked, trying to keep his cool in a ridiculously hot and steamy bathroom.

"Open up, I need my mascara!"

"I'll be out in a few minutes," he said, not wishing to end the privacy and pleasure he'd been enjoying.

"No, Caleb. I want it now. Hurry up!"

Reluctantly, he turned off the tap. The soap. Where was he going to put the soap so as not to ignite her suspicion? The guilt was debilitating.

After drying himself, Caleb tucked the soap in the towel and carried it in his hand. Opening the door, naked, he half smiled and said "the bathroom's all yours".

"What is that smell?" she demanded, looking around the steam-filled room. "It's like…it's like Christmas or something!"

"And how would you know what Christmas smells like when we don't celebrate it?"

Caleb was surprised by how abruptly the expression on her faced changed from accusation to being the accused. It was true that their religion didn't celebrate Christmas but they weren't immune to the cultural festivities in the world around them.

"What is the smell, Caleb?" she asked one more time with full awareness that it wasn't from anything she'd brought into their home.

"The scent is from some nice soap I picked up."

"Where did you get it?" she asked.

"Madge. It's soap. Why the thousand questions?"

"Because you've always used the Palmolive soap I've bought since the day we were married."

"I felt like a change. Now, if you don't mind, I need to get ready for work."

Saponification

As the simple piano melody of Debussy's Claire de Lune filled the studio that morning, Grace kept looking at the clock. Any minute Caleb would be knocking at the doors, rushing to get in out of the rain. Despite the blustery winds, she went to open them so he wouldn't need to get any more wet than necessary. Just as she turned the handle, he came into view, his dimpled smile embraced by the hood of his coat now lined with pendulous rain drops.

"Come in!" she said, inviting him inside.

"Bit of a wild morning," he replied, slipping out of his wet-weather clothes.

Grace could hardly take her eyes off him. He seemed so different to the man who first sat in her kitchen. Lighter, somehow. Happier.

"I'm just about to make a hot drink. Tea? Coffee?"

"That would be most welcome. Coffee, please. Black. I'll just start measuring up the curing racks while you're doing that."

"Okay," Grace said, setting two mugs to one side. "It was really good of you to fit this job in so quickly. I appreciate it."

"That's no problem. I have a few jobs on at the moment but I have flexibility around when I can do them. This is such a pleasant working environment that you have, Grace."

"Thanks. Beauty is important to me. I couldn't work in an office or somewhere with noise or harsh lighting or that just wasn't attractive."

"You don't mind working on your own?"

"Not at all. I used to..." she stopped, and

wondered how much she should share, but when she looked into his eyes Grace felt safe enough to give a little bit of herself away. "I used to have a studio shop in Australia that was on a busy seaside street. The tourists would come in and watch me and my mother work. We were business partners." Grace picked up the photo of Serena and passed it to Caleb.

"You look like twins!" he exclaimed.

"Everyone says that. Well, I always had company around whether it was Mum or the shoppers. Some days I miss all that but life changes us, doesn't it? These days I'm quite content just pottering about in the studio all day on my own. Besides, once Lilac gets in from school she doesn't stop chattering. I need all day in silence to get me through the few hours at the end of the day!" Grace laughed.

"Do you miss your mother?" Caleb asked.

Grace didn't reply straight away. It was a question which deserved a full and honest answer, but right now she just wanted to enjoy this friendly chat.

"More than you could ever imagine," she said, turning her back and pouring boiling water.

"What brought you to England?" Caleb asked.

"The short answer is: a change of perspective." It was time to get him talking. "Can I ask you something?"

"Of course," he said, putting down the tape measure and grabbing the coffee she offered him.

"I felt really angry the other day when Madge said not to worry about the environment. Do you really believe that Jehovah will just fix everything up?"

Looking downcast, Caleb sighed. "I don't know. There's a lot I don't know."

"Do you like being a Jehovah's Witness?"

"Like it?"

"Yeah, I mean, are you happy? Is it something you've chosen?"

"Grace, I've never had cause to question it," he said, then sipped slowly. "Until recently."

"It's just that you seem like a thoughtful person who probably does care about the environment. I mean, you do compost. That's a good start."

"I recycle, too!" he said, disarming her completely with his warm smile; then a shadow of doubt crept across his 48-hour unshaved jawline. "I struggle with not being allowed to question things. It's not encouraged. If I ask something that doesn't fit with the teachings, I'm cautioned. Those around me are quick to say 'apostate' in hushed tones. It's the quickest way to shut a dissenter up."

Caleb knew he was admitting too much, but it felt like a huge relief to actually talk to someone about his confusion, frustration and doubts.

"I'm not sure I understand. You mean you can't ask questions about the teachings?"

"Correct. The teachings are called The Truth."

"If there was any validity to the teachings, then surely it would stand up to scrutiny?" Grace said, placing her mug on the bench. "Otherwise, you know, it's mind control." She wondered now if she'd gone too far but Caleb nodded in agreement.

"So why stay?" she asked, perplexed that he remained mired in the religion. "You're not a tree, Caleb. You're not stuck." Grace could have kicked herself. It was wrong to dish out advice to a complete stranger.

"If only it were that simple."

"Yes, it is. Just leave."

"It's not, Grace. All my friends, my community,

my family are all Jehovah's Witnesses. If I was to walk away, I'd be shunned."

"Shunned? What do you mean?"

"Every member of my community would have to cut me from their lives and cease all communication until I came back to my senses. My whole life has been involved in this organisation. If I walk away, I have nothing. No friends, no family."

"Your friends and family would just stop talking to you, Caleb? Surely not!"

"Yes, Grace, they would. It's part of their spiritual duty or responsibility."

"That's bloody ridiculous!" she said, trying to imagine what it was like to live within that level of control.

"Yes, but can you imagine what it would be like to start your life over again with absolutely no one in it?"

Grace knew exactly what that felt like. She had Lilac, of course, but it was just the two of them starting their lives over. Alone.

"I'm sorry Caleb. I'm sorry that you're in this position."

"Thanks for the coffee, Grace. I'll get back to work."

As she took the mug from him, their hands brushed and she felt a rush rip through her body.

"You won't be alone, Caleb. I know we don't really know each other, but I won't stop talking to you."

There was that half smile again. She'd come to notice he did it a lot as if he wasn't sure about something and was half-heartedly nodding in agreement just to keep the peace. *Years of practice,* she decided.

Drops of rain slid down the windows, and as the morning continued Caleb measured and wrote down building plans. They worked in the studio in quiet companionship to the sound of the rain, the click of his tape measure, classical piano music, and Grace's stick blender punctuating air. When Grace turned off the blender, the scent of jasmine caught Caleb's attention and he asked her about the soapmaking process.

"My favourite part is when I add the lye-water to the oils and turn the stick blender on. It's quite meditative really. There's a real sense of magic as the blended mixture turns, ever so slowly, from the bottom of the bowl upwards. It's thick, creamy and swirly. At first the bowl is just a mixture of oils but soon it looks like melted butter."

"A bit like cooking, then?" he asked, listening intently to every word.

"In a way, I suppose. It's a slow process. When the oils and butters are blended, I add in any extras like flowers, fruits, berries, leaves and so on, and stir them through with the wooden paddle."

"The lye? Caustic soda, right?"

"Yeah, but it's saponified. A chemical reaction happens in the process of soapmaking and it's neutralised."

"Sounds more like science than baking!"

"Either way, it's often a case of trial and error when I'm working on a new soap. Chemistry is important," she said, looking deeply into his blue eyes. "A good batch is heavenly. It's just the right combination of colours and scent. The blend should be smooth and similar to cake batter. If you end up making a bad batch it's all sticky like biscuit dough. It's highly frustrating. I can't sell those ones."

"What do you do with them?"

"Lilac! She loves any of the soaps I can't sell. You should see her collection! Anything can cause a batch to be bad. Trying to figure out what the variable is can be time consuming. It might be that a particular oil hasn't worked well with the lye. It takes a lot of time to get the oils just right and then adding scents and colourants. And there's a heck of a lot of blending to be done. At every stage I'm trying to remember what I've done so I can scribble down my recipe. And then, it takes about four to six weeks for a batch of soap to cure."

"It sounds so labour intensive."

"Sure is. And then when I do create a really fabulous soap I'm reluctant to sell it. I get quite protective over the good batches," she admitted, passing him a bar of wild violet and honey soap to smell.

Caleb smiled, unwilling to break the flow of conversation, and reluctantly said "I'm just heading out to the van to bring in some wood."

After he slid into his raincoat, he raced up the garden. Grace watched him. It was so easy having him around. *Careful Grace, don't get too used to him. He's not yours.*

When he returned, Grace said "I'm just popping into the house to heat some soup for lunch. Would you like to join me? There's plenty."

Caleb looked up with delight.

"I wasn't expecting you to feed me."

"It's no problem. There's plenty. Come on. Let's eat." She led him through an interior door to the house, and once in the kitchen he stood by the sink while she prepared things.

Grace made smalltalk but was aware the whole time that he was studying the kitchen; the books on her shelves, and the glass jars filled with nuts, seeds and legumes, the dried herbs hanging from hooks in the ceiling, plaits of garlic strung up by the Aga, and bowls of colourful fruits and baskets of root vegetables. Lilac's drawings covered an entire wall.

Setting the soup bowls onto the table, Grace then placed the basket of miniature bread rolls between them, and lay down some cutlery and linen napkins.

"Courgette and leek soup. Is that okay?"

"Smells gorgeous!"

Just as Caleb was washing his hands at the Irish porcelain sink, his mobile phone rang. Grace watched him fumble as he retrieved the phone from his pocket, then hit 'reject'.

"Feel free to take your call, Caleb. I can cover this and keep it warm."

"No, it can wait. I didn't realise how hungry I was. Thank you."

The phone vibrated in his pocket. Grace watched as he dunked his bread roll into the soup.

"You're a fabulous cook, Grace."

Buzzzzz

Buzzzzz

Buzzzzz

Grace could hear the phone vibrating. "It must be important. Whoever it is, they're being persistent."

"Madge."

"Oh. And you don't want to talk to your wife?"

He shrugged his shoulders as if to say 'not really', and then reached for his phone, and moving a bit away from the table, called her back.

Grace could hear Madge's demanding tone.

"Why didn't you answer your phone?"

"I'm working. What can I help you with?" he asked kindly in stark contrast to her aggression.

"Ciara and Arthur need chaperoning tonight but I've got Bible study with the Harrisons. Tonight we're talking about the Garden of Eden."

Grace hated eavesdropping but Madge's voice was so loud that even with the phone to Caleb's ear, it was still audible.

"No, Madge. I chaperoned them last night and many, many nights before. It's your turn. They don't have to spend every single night together."

Caleb waved his phone in the air. Grace thought he'd lost mobile signal then realised Madge had hung up on him.

"I've chaperoned almost every night for the past three weeks. It was time to put my foot down," he said quietly, returning to the table.

"Chaperone? Sounds a bit old fashioned, Caleb."

"It is. If it's so important to the congregation that my daughter shouldn't be alone with her boyfriend until marriage, then someone else needs to start shouldering the responsibility."

Grace sensed the unfamiliar feeling of liberation washing over him as he turned the phone off and put it into his work belt.

The soap must be working.

They chatted through lunch, sharing conversations about gardening, the Cumbrian weather and their children.

"That lunch was amazing, Grace. Thank you!"

"My pleasure."

Grace thought better than to quiz him any more about his religion. He'd already been open and uninhibited with every question she'd asked.

As the work day neared its end, and Grace began to get ready for the school run, Caleb turned around and said "One curing rack now complete. What do you think, Grace?"

"It's perfect!" Grace said, running her fingers along the smooth edges, grateful it was complete but aware that he'd finish the others before too long. And then, he'd be gone. Gone from her life forever.

Extinct

Madge slammed the drawers shut. Where the hell was the damn soap? She scoured every square inch of the bedroom: digging in the back of drawers, weeding items out of the wardrobe, moving the mattress, peering beneath Caleb's pillow, shaking out the inside of his shoes, beneath the blanket box, as well as every compartment in the bathroom. The scent lingered in her nostrils, taunting her. It was everywhere but nowhere!

Madge had promised to meet Deb in five minutes so they could go out on the ministry in Carlisle city centre, but she was determined to find the soap first.

Caleb was driving Ciara to her Saturday morning job at a local coffee shop. Madge was grateful to have him out of the house for a short time. Maybe he'd hidden it in the garden shed? After all, he spent a lot of his spare time in there.

After finding the right key, she unlocked the wooden building. One by one, she pulled out all of his tool boxes, potting trays, storage containers. Where did he hide it? Even though she knew it wasn't in the shed she turned everything upside down anyway. There was no sign or scent of it. Where could he have put it? Why didn't he leave it in the shower? Unsettled, Madge strode back into the house and snatched up her handbag. With a quick strip of lipstick across her lips, she then brushed her long black hair. It didn't make sense: at one level it felt like her life was falling apart and yet nothing had happened. Nothing at all. It was just a bar of soap.

She jumped, then answered the shrill ring of her phone. "Yes, Deb, I'm on my way. See you soon."

The ten-minute drive into the city centre gave her some private moments to gather her erratic thoughts and put them into some order. With each stop at a red light, she tilted the rear-vision mirror to examine her face. *I'm still attractive, aren't I?* She studied the bleed lines coming from her poppy-red lipstick. *He still desires me, doesn't he?* Madge searched her memory, and tried to remember the last time they'd made love. *Has it been weeks or months? When was the last time he held me in his arms? Or paid me a compliment? When did he last kiss me like a lover rather than on my forehead like I'm an aging aunty?*

The angry toot of a horn from the car behind urged her on.

After finding a space in the carpark, and memorising its location, Madge headed down the lifts by the public library. Barely present in her own body, she wandered by the shops in the Lanes Shopping Centre in what was a never-ending trek to get to English Street. The scent of exotic perfumes mingled with freshly-cooked donuts, but for Madge, there was nothing sweet about the morning. Nothing at all. Even the dimple-cheeked toddlers made no impression on her.

There, opposite Costa, Deb had already set up their trolley for the day and was passing a Watchtower magazine to an interested pedestrian.

"Hi Deb, sorry I'm late."

"Are you alright, Madge? You look a bit flustered."

"Yeah, I'm fine. Just got held up. Have you handed out many magazines yet?"

"No, just that one. Sure glad it's not raining today. By the way, there's a march coming through here shortly. Hopefully it won't impact what we're doing too much."

"Is that the environmental march?" Madge groaned, suddenly remembering Grace was at the forefront. Uncomfortable at the memory of their heated discussion, she twisted her wedding ring as was her habit whenever life felt unkind. Somehow that band of gold gave her surety in an uncertain world. If there was anything she could rely on, it was marriage for life: one person to always be there for you no matter what.

"Extinction Rebellion. I think that's what it's called. I don't imagine many people will go to it," Deb said.

Madge settled herself beside Deb and, as they caught up with each other's news, she stopped listening and wondered if Jehovah had forgotten her. There, amongst the nauseating cigarette fumes and the tangy aroma of hot chips drenched in vinegar, she felt terribly alone in the world. Deb chatted nonstop, just as she usually did, but Madge barely took in a word.

It was a little before noon when Madge first heard them: a cacophony of ringing bells, the banging of drums, shaking of rattles and shrill whistles. Each sound, specifically designed to alert the shoppers, soon had everyone turning their heads to observe the spectacle before them.

Colourful banners were what she noticed next: posters and flags waving high above the moving crowd.

Madge regretted coming out on the information trolleys this morning. It wasn't that she found Grace unpleasant, but more about how determined she'd been that the Earth needed saving. It was at odds with everything Madge was taught as a Jehovah's Witness. If she was honest, she was still angry at Caleb for sitting on the fence about composting. And now she was even angrier because he smelt of Christmas!

To Madge's surprise, the crowd was huge. Like a rotund caterpillar that'd gorged on too many long lunches, it inched its way up English Street, a colourful stream of over one thousand people, from all around Cumbria, urgently brandishing placards pleading with people to take environmental responsibility.

It wasn't hard to pick Grace out in the crowd. As she led the way, her wavy copper hair glistened in the morning sunlight. Madge wanted to turn away, and avoid being seen by Grace, but Deb was so busy chatting to her that it would have been rude to break off the conversation. Not that she could get a word in edgeways, anyway.

As the crowd drew closer, Madge couldn't help compare herself to Grace. She wondered if Grace ever wore makeup. Somehow she seemed comfortable in her own skin and it was as if she didn't feel the need to accentuate any features. They spoke for themselves.

Madge always wore skirts, blouses and jackets, and dressed immaculately at all times of the day, even when she never left the house.

Studying Grace in her faded denim jeans and purple t-shirt, walking alongside a young girl with the same shade of copper hair and facial features, Madge wondered why Grace's husband wasn't marching. Maybe he was further back in the crowd?

When their eyes met, Grace smiled and said "Hi Madge! Here, have one of these flyers."

"No thanks," Madge said firmly, realising she was being rude but to the point.

Grace said "But I read The Watchtower, cover to cover, surely you can reciprocate?" Her words were softly spoken.

Madge could feel Deb's eyes going back and forth between them, surprised they knew each other. Reluctantly, she took the flyer, determined to ditch it in the bin the second Grace was out of sight. Madge was surprised that Grace was still smiling despite the way she'd spoken to her.

"Have a nice day, Madge," she said as she continued to lead the way.

Madge looked at Deb. "What? What's that look for, Deb?"

"Why were you so terse with that woman? Who is she?"

Suddenly it hit Madge. The scent lingering from Grace. Not the same as Caleb's soap; not the same at all, but yet there was something familiar about it. If soaps were related, then they were sisters! It wasn't even that she could say what it was, but it didn't smell the same as any soap she'd ever known. As if someone had punched her in the belly, Madge wondered if Caleb and Grace had ever seen each other apart from the day when they'd gone door-to-door pioneering. *No, of course they hadn't. Why would they?*

Deb browsed through the flyer and, much to Madge's annoyance, read out loud: "A global environmental movement, the aim of the Extinction Rebellion is to use non-violent civil disobedience to compel the government to act urgently."

Madge was barely taking in any of the words. Suddenly, she said to Deb, "I don't feel well. I'm going home. Sorry. You'll be fine on your own."

Without a backwards glance, Madge elbowed her way through the slow-moving march, mumbling "Excuse me" with every laboured step across the street. There were so many people: adults holding hands with young children, rowdy teenagers, and gurgling babies. Calls of 'save the environment' and 'act before it's too late' bombarded her. It was like being in another world. A nightmare. Madge hated every second of it and prayed to Jehovah to show her the way back to the carpark.

Twenty minutes later, much to her relief, she pulled into the driveway. As she opened the car door, the aroma of freshly cut grass should have felt welcoming, like home, like her safe place, but today it stunk of betrayal. For a moment, she stood by the car and watched Caleb mowing the lawn, intently focused on each length parallel to the fence line. Madge headed over and when she caught his eye motioned for him to cut the engine.

"Where did you get the soap?" she demanded when the motor died down.

"The soap?" he asked. "What do you mean where did I get it? Why are you so obsessed about me using a different soap than I've used for eighteen years? Is there a law about what soap I have to use now?"

Angry that he was trying to put the question back on her shoulders, she slapped him across the cheek.

"Are you having an affair with that tree-hugger woman?"

Holding his hand to the sting stretching itself across his face, Caleb shook his head.

"Madge, you're being ridiculous! What's got into you? No, I'm not having an affair. Any more questions?

Can I get back to mowing?"

As Madge studied his eyes, she realised he was telling the truth. For a moment, she didn't know whether to be angry or relieved.

"I'm simply trying a different soap." Caleb looked out across the field adjacent to their home, with newborn lambs gambolling about, and then sighed. "I picked it up the other day at the garden centre when I bought some potting mix. Why are you back from the trolleys so soon?" he asked, facing her again.

Madge turned, leaving his question unanswered. Half-way back to the house she spun around.

"Where did you put the soap?" she asked.

"It's in the shower. Where else would it be?"

Ethics

Grace switched on the laptop, and while waiting for it to start up sipped her ginger tea. It felt odd that Caleb wasn't in the studio today, and nor had he been for the past week. Although she knew he had other clients, she'd gotten used to his company, gentle humour and quiet ways, and how he'd often break into a whistle; a sure sign he was happy. In some ways, when he was in the room, it was like he wasn't even there: it was the highest compliment she could have paid him. It suited her introvert ways when she was with people who didn't jangle her nerves too much with their loud and busy presence. *At least he'll be back on Monday*, she told herself. *Four more days to go.*

Grace distracted herself from the gnawing ache in her belly. *He's not yours*, she told herself more than once that morning. At least updating her blog would keep her focused for a while until she began her next batch of soaps. Ethics, she typed into the header.

At Dragonfly Soaps a conscious approach is taken to the ethics of this creative business. For example, there is no palm oil, no plastic packaging, and no animal testing.

Her fingers remained still on the keyboard. *Ethics*, she wondered. *Why invest so strongly in them in her business, but send Caleb home with soaps that she knew would change his life?* Even though the recipient of any of her soaps had free will, the botanical compounds awakened them to possibilities and choices. And choice, she knew, was where the potentiality of human life found its purpose.

"Choice," she said out loud. "Choice".

Follow The Scent

For the past few weeks, Madge had noticed some new varieties of soap appearing in the shower. It took all her restraint not to mention them to Caleb, and she was also surprised that he didn't attempt to hide them. Was he trying to arouse her suspicion? Despite what he said, she was 100% sure that he had hidden the Christmas-scented soap despite it apparently being in the shower all along.

It was the latest soap which wrangled her nerves: Grapefruit and Poppy Seed. Madge had to admit the citrus scent was intoxicating, and it was an interesting combination. Not that she used any of the soaps Caleb brought home, but she was intrigued, each time, to see what they smelled like. The truth was it did make the bathroom feel more welcoming each time she went in there.

The wrapper was discarded in the bathroom bin, but part of the label had been ripped off just revealing the name of the soap. Where did it come from? Where did any of these soaps come from? Madge checked the time, and made some mental calculations as to how she'd spend the rest of the day.

Caleb had sourced his gardening supplies from Houghton Garden Centre since it first opened in 2006. On the odd occasion, Madge came along for the ride, not to look at plants or compost, but to have a cup of tea and scone in the café and a look through the gift shop. As far as she could recall, she'd never noticed soaps in there before but then she'd never thought to look for them. As she pulled off the motorway at junction 44, she took the last exit down towards the garden centre.

Upon arrival, she was frustrated to see the carpark was almost full. Finally, there was a vacant spot. Once she'd parked and turned off the engine, Madge pulled the mirror around to examine her face. There was never any question that she was the prettiest girl in the congregation, but that was 18 years ago. What now? Had life dulled her looks? Had Caleb stopped seeing her for the beauty she was? What had changed?

The foundation of her life was shifting at an alarming rate: an ill mother, a daughter desperate to leave home and marry, and a husband who was emotionally absent. Perhaps all this stress was aging her far too quickly?

The soap collection was small, just four varieties. They certainly had a lovely scent, but none of them resembled what Caleb had been using, and besides, they were different in shape and the label didn't match. Madge noticed the scent of each one was distinctive but none of them drew her in in the same way Caleb's soaps had. If she didn't know better, Madge would think his soaps had their own personality. *Don't be stupid, Madge!*

When a staff member wandered by, dusting shelves and moving things around, Madge questioned them about the soaps.

"No. These are the only ones we stock in the store. It's only ever been this range, and this size. I've worked here for years. I'm the one who orders them in. Honestly, there haven't been any others."

"Ok," Madge replied, unconvinced. If the assistant was telling the truth, then it could only mean one thing: that Caleb had lied to her about the soap. This was the only garden centre he ever came to. If the soap wasn't from here, then where was it from? Had he bought it, or had someone given it to him?

In her exasperation, Madge purchased one of each soap: rose; lavender; vanilla; geranium.

Once she was home, she placed them in a basket by the bathroom basin. Quickly, she opened the geranium soap, and breathed it in. It wasn't just that it was a different plant than the ones Caleb used, but the scent had a different—she couldn't find the word at first—*feel*. It felt different, and that meant she felt different. As she washed her hands, slowly at first, the scent pervaded the bathroom. Suds gurgled down the sink, away, far away, from the sadness she felt. If she didn't know better, she'd have thought her marriage was disintegrating and she had no way to stop it. In fury, she grabbed the scrubbing brush and rubbed back and forward until her skin was red raw. As she scrubbed around her wedding ring, remembering the day they took their vows at the Kingdom Hall, she yelled: "We're meant to be together forever!" It was only the ring of her mobile phone that had her tumbling out of the frantic scrubbing. The words *Chell is calling you* flashed upon the screen. Why was her mother phoning?

"Mum, what is it? Are you okay? Do you need me?" she asked, putting it onto speaker phone and then dabbing the blood from her wrists.

"I've been thinking about your offer," Chell said. "I will move in with you. If that's still okay? If Caleb is in agreement."

Madge didn't care if Caleb agreed or not. If Caleb had lied to her about the soap, what else was he keeping from her?

"That's great, Mum. Don't worry about Caleb. Everything's fine."

Madge ended the call and placed the soap on the shower holder, still perplexed that one soap manufacturer could create a soap so different from another.

Grapefruit & Poppy Seed Soap

Our Maker told us that our job, our one and only mission, was to imbue our person with the ability to release the confusion which happens when there is endless chatter in the mind. Our job is to cast love upon mind, body and soul; to bring cleansing to the whole being. As we are held, and utilised for what might seem an everyday purpose, we're programmed to infuse love, especially if there have been years of self-neglect. Our Maker paired grapefruit with poppy seeds to encourage the beholder with a bright future. We work together seamlessly.

There's another soap waiting beside us in our person's shower today, but we instinctively know that it hasn't been crafted by our Maker. It sings no songs, speaks no stories. We'd go so far as to say it is mute. There is no life. And it is certainly not imbued with any invocation. Perhaps this is what our Maker means when she tells us we're special.

Cumbrian Soap Collection

Grace was listening to Caleb's Cumbrian accent and how it played upon her ear. It was so far removed from her native Australian. It was a strong dialectical accent, with a smattering of the old language, and the more he spoke, the more homesick she felt. So far away from familiar soils.

I need rooting. I need to be grounded to this place, this land. I've chosen to make this my home, and so to the Earth I must return so she can hold me.

When their conversation came to a natural end, and they both continued with their jobs: him measuring, calculating and sawing; her cutting loaves of soap, an idea came to her.

Grace walked over to her polished-oak workbench, grabbed a notepad, and looked through various notes she'd made from expeditions with Lilac along the Cumbrian coastline, fields, fells, bogs and marshes. And slowly, the seeds of an idea came to her in a vision, with complete clarity. Soon she began writing furiously, as if she had a shopping list and was deciding what recipes to make. It hadn't occurred to Grace that her feelings were visible on her face.

"You look happy," Caleb said, putting his tape measure down.

"I am, actually. I've just had an idea that's so obvious I'm surprised I've not thought of it before."

"Care to share?" he asked.

She thought for a moment, and then said "In Australia, I was so familiar with the flora all around me, and for miles and miles around me. I knew where I was from. I was connected. And here, in your homeland, and your county, I'm a transplant. I'm out of place. I don't know this land, and I need to befriend it. Sure, I am familiar with what I grow here in the garden or conservatory, but out there in the wild landscape, not so much. Lilac and I have done plenty of exploring this past couple of years, and I have lots of sketches in my notebooks and have done plenty of research, but it doesn't come naturally to me. Do you know what I mean?"

"Yes, I think so."

"So, I'm looking at my notes and realising I could create a range of soaps that are specifically Cumbrian."

"What do you have in mind?"

"Do you really want to hear?"

"Of course!"

Grace was delighted to have someone to bounce ideas off. This had become such a solitary job, a stark contrast to all the years by her mother's side where they shared ideas every day.

"So, these are some of the plants I've learned about, and in some cases what I might pair it up with. It's an incomplete list but it would be a good start to Cumbrian-specific soaps."

She read out of her list:

Fellside Wild Lavender
Seaweed and Celandine
Yellow Star of Bethlehem
Cumbrian Moss
Wild Nettle and Heather
Bog Bilberry
Primrose and Wild White Orchid
Alpine Forget-Me-Not
Rock Samphire
Violet

"And that's all just come to you while you were sitting there sipping your tea?"

"Yeah, you could say that!"

They both laughed, and then Caleb added: "I've never been around such a creative woman."

"Madge isn't creative?"

"Madge's life revolves around going out on the trolleys and passing out copies of The Watchtower, and cleaning the house."

"Cleaning the house is creative," Grace added. "If you have the right sort of music playing and you can dance while you mop," she laughed.

"Grace, you strike me as a person who is content in their own skin."

"How do you mean?"

"Well, you know, some people can be high maintenance. And others are low maintenance. But from what I can see, you're self-maintaining. You seem happy with your life. It's almost like you don't need anybody."

"Life is what you make it, right?" She smiled, and decided not to continue the conversation. "I'll carry on with my notes," she said, and then added "Let me know if you need anything."

Botanical Additives

After Grace had caught up with her soapmaking for the day, and tidied her workspace, she decided to dedicate some time to updating her blog. In a fairly short time, she'd attracted quite a following of soapers, both beginners and professional, who not only enjoyed her offerings on the soapmaking process but were rather taken with the philosophical whisperings written in each post. Not that she ever intended for it to be that way. The blog was nothing more than a way of making sure the website ranked high in internet searches. She soon found, however, that writing down her thoughts became a reflective practice, and there were dozens of comments left after each post.

> The choice of which botanicals to add to my soap includes plant extracts, dried plants, infusions, roots, clays, oils like hemp seed, grape seed, liquid wax like jojoba. How often do we consider what we add to our own lives?

She looked over at Caleb, busy in his work, and was grateful for his quiet and gentle presence not only in the studio but, she realised, in her life.

> Do they help or hinder, detract or encourage? Why do we choose anything? Or anyone? A soap is functional.

It has, for the most part, one purpose: to clean. When I create soap, obviously there is great care taken in *how* it will clean. Is it a soap which will lather well? Am I choosing a base of ingredients which are perhaps creamy and moisturising? These decisions, while creative, still lean towards the functional aspect of soap: its purpose.

Once my foundation is in place, then I look at the features: botanical additions, colour and scent. For me, this is a creative playground. So much time and reflection go into these choices. Will I combine two flowers or use just one and add an essential oil? Will I add a natural plant-based colouring or will the plants I'm using generate enough colour on their own?

I've discovered that there is no end to the combinations I can create. To be clear, it is in the feature element of soapmaking where I really come alive.

And what of life itself? What are our functional needs and featured desires? Do we place value on the

latter, or do we 'make do' and
just get by? Is it enough to have
a roof over our head and food
in the pantry? What of family?
Friendship? And what of love?
Functional or feature? Or maybe
they're both.

Perhaps the difference between
a ho-hum life and an amazing,
charmed life is like the difference
between unscented basic soap and
the soaps lovingly handcrafted
here at Dragonfly Cottage.
Scentually Yours, Grace x

"You look pleased with yourself," Caleb said, noticing the smile on her face as she closed the lid of the laptop.

"I suppose I am," she said. "Let me ask you something, Caleb. What is the most important thing in your life? The thing you can't do without?"

"Is this a trick question?" he laughed. "Rather deep for this time of day, don't you think? Have you been writing one of your philosophical blogs again?"

"You read my blogs?" she asked, surprised that he would have even been on her website.

"I had to check that I wasn't working for someone who was maybe a bit crazy."

"Well, now that you've ascertained my sanity, are you going to answer the question?"

"I'm still undecided on whether you're crazy or not" he smiled. "As for your question, no one has ever asked me that before, Grace."

"But you must have thought it?" she replied.

"I suppose protecting my family from harm."

"Yes, I can understand that. It's primal, isn't it?"

"I don't suppose that's what you were really getting at though. Do you mean what is the thing I need most in my life?"

"Yeah. You know, apart from a house and food."

"These days I wonder what it is we ever truly need. Perhaps we've become so disconnected from nature that we forget the Earth has everything," he said.

"You're right about that. All our food, medicines, and even shelter is there if only we open our eyes and see."

"I've been taught not to need anything but to follow Jehovah. I don't know what I need."

"What about what you desire?"

"Aren't they really the same thing in the end?" Caleb asked, hoping for clarity.

"Maybe you're right."

"I desire inner peace. To be able to sleep at night and not worry.

"And?"

"Do you always ask so many questions, Grace?"

She laughed. "I'm just curious. I like to know what makes people tick, and what they yearn for. What makes someone bounce out of bed in the morning with a yearning passion for life?"

"I can't remember the last time I bounced out of bed, Grace, but I suspect you do every single morning? I can't imagine you living any other way."

"I do, as it happens. I look forward to each day and wonder with excitement just what it will bring."

"The last time I had that amount of joy was

probably when I was seventeen and went off camping with my mates down in the Lake District."

"And you've just been ticking along since then?"

"You could say that, yes."

"Don't you want more? Isn't there a part of you that craves pleasure, fun, creativity, adventure? That lad who went camping all those years ago, he's still in there, Caleb. He really is."

"Oh, Grace, if only my life were as simple as yours, then yes, maybe I would be that enthusiastic. I watch you, and the way you live, and how you mother Lilac, and your passion for protecting the Earth, and I really admire it. I find it attractive and magnetic, but for me, it all seems so out of reach."

"So, you're just going to tread water for the rest of your life?"

A silence settled over them when the reality of Grace's question landed with him.

"I'll make us a cuppa," Grace said, disrupting their unspoken thoughts. "Caleb, no matter what your life looks like now or what you've always known, you're only ever one decision away from a completely different life. And that decision, that choice, doesn't even have to be huge."

"Grace, what about you? What's the most important thing in your life? Besides Lilac, of course."

"Freedom."

"And do you feel free?"

Oil and Water Don't Mix

It was a sunny afternoon when a knock at the conservatory door startled both of them. A courier, with a beaming smile, motioned to two boxes at his feet. Grace walked over, and let him in.

"Thanks!"

"Four more boxes in the van, love", he said.

"I'll help," Caleb offered, and within a couple of minutes all six boxes were on Grace's work bench.

"An order of oils from my supplier," she said, opening the boxes one at a time.

"Can I help with anything?" Caleb asked.

"Sure, that'd be great. I'll call out what I've got, and if you could tick them off the delivery note that would help a lot," she said as she reached in, taking out bottle after bottle, and placing them inside a wooden cupboard.

"Five bottles of sweet almond oil."

"Yes."

"Three bottles of castor oil."

"Yes."

"Ten kilograms of coconut oil."

"Yes."

"Four buckets of coconut butter."

"Yes."

"Seven bottles of apricot-kernel oil."

"Yes."

"Bored yet?" she laughed.

"Not at all."

"Four bottles of argan oil, and four of avocado oil."

"Double yes."

They both smiled at each other, and Grace could have kicked herself for the delicious feeling which swept throughout her whole being. *Did he feel it too?*

"Two flaxseed, two evening primrose and two safflower oil."

"A hattrick of yesses."

And again, that smile. How could a single smile turn your world upside down and inside out?

"Four bottles of rosehip oil, and a 5kg bucket of mango butter."

"Both here on the list," he said, ticking them off. "It's a lovely thing you do in this world, Grace. Making soap."

"I like to think I'm dispensing scented beauty in a tangible form."

"You're definitely doing that, but it's something else too that I can't put my finger on. That soap you gave me?" he said, hesitating.

"Yes?" she answered, feeling alarmed. Did he guess the secret ingredients? Could he possibly know that her soaps went way beyond being an item for cleansing the body?

"This might sound odd…"

"Go on," she encouraged.

"I feel different. I'm thinking differently. It's… never mind. It sounds silly!"

"No, Caleb. It's not silly. Not silly at all. Tell me."

"That soap is changing my life. That does sound stupid, right?"

Grace didn't answer. She couldn't lie and say "It's just soap", but could she tell him the truth? Her soaps were agents of change aligning people to their future selves.

"Tell me how your life is changing, Caleb?"

"For years, I've felt shackled, and now all the things that have constrained me…well, it's like I can see them for who and what they are, and I want to be free of them. I feel desperate to untangle myself from anything that's ever held me back."

"And will you be free of them or are you just thinking about it?"

"I'm changing, Grace. Changing from the inside and I'm not sure yet how the outside will change but everything seems so different. I don't even know who I am anymore."

"Well, you seem lighter than the man I met that day at the top of the garden." She smiled, then filled the kettle. "Another cuppa?"

"Sure," he said, measuring another piece of dowel.

"This one life is precious, Grace, and being around you each day is showing me that more and more. It's like you hold the magic of life in your hands and you value it in a way I've never seen anyone do before."

"Thank you, Caleb. That's so kind."

"No, thank you, Grace. Thank you. I've grown up with a faith system called The Truth, that says Paradise is coming, and yet when I look at you and your life it's like you've already created Paradise here on Earth. You even live in a Garden of Eden."

"Now is all anyone has, Caleb. Just now. There's no tomorrow, no magical nirvana. Sure, it exists, but it's up to us to make it our current reality. That's my truth, anyway."

"I feel that trying to fit in with the life I've always known, and the person I'm becoming or would like to be, is like mixing oil and water."

I Spy

Madge watched Caleb leave the driveway, then she stepped outside into her second-hand powder-blue Mini Cooper and slowly pulled into the road.

Where was he working these days? Not once had Caleb mentioned what jobs he was doing, or which part of town he was in, and yet he seemed to be working more than part time. These days, he never seemed to have time for knocking on doors or going on trolleys, and once or twice had said he was too tired to do Bible study or go to a meeting. Although she knew that she should have just asked him, after the soap situation when she searched high and low, indoors and outdoors, day and night, only for it to miraculously be in the shower 'all along', she wasn't sure she could trust him at all. Better to play him at his own game. For five days now, she'd followed him when he left for work. Each time he'd been at the McEnry Farm off Durdar Road, and yet her gut still didn't trust him. Today, she watched his car, about a hundred metres or so ahead, with just one car in between them, weave its way along the road, until it veered out of the area and down into a village, and then another village, and so on for many miles. *Odd, he really didn't mention anything about travelling out of town to work.* And then a pang in her gut. Wasn't this near to where that environmental activist lived? Madge watched his car turn down a no-through road. No. surely not? Why was he going there? What should she do? Follow him down? Was he working there? Surely he wouldn't go door knocking on his own? Was he having an affair?

Madge's mouth felt dry. Nothing in her life had prepared her for this god-awful moment. Where was her Jehovah? Why would Caleb do this?

For three hours, she sat motionless waiting for the return of his car. Nothing. No car. No sign of him. *Should I drive down?* If she did, what might she see?

Eventually, she could stand it no longer and pulled out her phone and texted:

> Caleb, are you home
> for lunch?

When there was no reply after half an hour, Madge wiped a tear from the corner of her eye. As she looked at the landscape in the rear-view mirror, she wondered what would become of her and Caleb. All these years of marriage behind them, and she realised, for the first time, that she didn't know him at all. A quiet sob escaped her lips. She texted again:

> Caleb, are you coming
> home for lunch?

Why wasn't he answering? Was he having sex with her? Did he even have his phone with him? Was it switched on? She texted Ciara.

> Ciara, can you text your Dad
> and see where he is?

Ten minutes, later, Madge's phone beeped.

> He's not answered.
> Don't know where he is Mum.
> Why?

> Nothing. Don't worry.

She'd call him. He'd have to pick up. Madge dialled his number. No answer.

For the next half an hour, she hit 'dial' on repeat.

Inch by inch, she drove down the country lane. As she pulled up by the side of his pick-up truck, there was no sight of him. When she looked inside the cab, she saw his phone on the dashboard. What was he doing inside the house?

Whatever he was doing, he certainly didn't want to be disturbed.

Madge returned to her car and reversed several metres until she could back into the open gateway of a field, and then turned around, her face stripped of colour, and drove home. Alone.

Bog Bilberry

Despite the peaceful and pleasant morning that they'd shared in each other's company, and the laughter over lunchtime, dining on roasted red pepper and tomato soup with olive-bread croutons, by mid-afternoon Grace didn't feel right. It wasn't anything she could identify. Caleb continued to calculate and cut, on repeat, and whistle a tune here and there, clearly happy in his work. But Grace felt as if a dark cloud had descended over her home. What forces were at work? This was her safe place in the world, her sanctuary from life's storms, and yet...and yet, she was distinctively out of place.

Every muscle began to twitch. Grace brewed a pot of chamomile tea to steady her nerves, and then researched her notes. *I need protecting.* Then she looked over at Caleb. *We need protecting.* At every turn she'd been careful to disguise her identity, and cover her tracks. The authorities had allowed Lilac to travel under her passport in the name of Grace Lysander rather than as Lilac. *What storm was brewing?*

A shiver ran up her spine, and she brushed her hands over the goosebumps on her arms.

Her notes read:

Bilberry
Protects against lightning strikes
and protects the house.

A thought occurred to Grace, and she turned to Caleb.

"Does Madge know you're working here?"

"Madge?"

"Yes, Madge, your wife?"

"No."

"Why?"

"Why would she? I don't tell her where I go to work."

"Would she find it odd?"

Caleb sighed. "I can't imagine she'd be happy that I was in a house alone, all day, with…"

"With?"

"A beautiful woman."

Grace placed her hand on her cheek, feeling the warmth rise.

"Is she the jealous type?"

"I've never given her cause to be jealous."

"Don't give her cause now, Caleb," she warned, her tone gentle but firm.

"Are you suggesting I tell her or not tell her?"

"It would be better to find out from you sooner rather than later, don't you think?"

"Yes. You're right."

"I'm sure you've worked for other women before?"

Caleb thought about it for a moment, and then said "Yes, of course I have. It's just that, well, they were from within the Jehovah's Witnesses community. Sisters. That's what we call them. Madge would never think twice about me going and doing work in their homes and spending time alone with a sister."

"So the issue with me, or rather the reason you've not told her you're here, is because I'm not part of your community?"

"Yes. Mostly."

"Mostly?"

"You're not exactly an elderly spinster past your prime, Grace!"

They both laughed.

"Right, we both better get back to work," Grace suggested. And then she knew what to do, what had to be done, for both their sakes.

Grace recalled a place which had become special to her during her time in England. Quite early on, she'd befriended another school mum whose family were hill farmers. They'd offered her free access to their land, and she made the most of any opportunity to ramble fields and fells further away from her own land.

It was in June, when they first caught her attention with their small, pink bell-shaped flowers. And just two months later, when she returned, the bushes were covered in bilberries. That morning, she and Lilac feasted, noticing the flesh of the fruit was red rather than white like blueberries. The low bilberry bushes, with solitary fruits of blue-black, were found in abundance. Lilac frolicked amongst the bushes then settled herself down to study the soft mosses and insects at her feet.

Grace had been wild harvesting roots, leaves, mosses, barks and berries her whole life, and waited until a plant called to her. Not once did she ever take without asking. As she listened to the voice of the bilberries, it was as if they were singing in chorus: *Hang branches of us in your home*, they said. *We'll guard against lightning strikes.*

That morning she knew that one day she'd want them for soap. The weather turned sharply. What began as a perfectly sunny 'butter wouldn't melt in its mouth' kind of day, ended up driving them back down the hill with a storm unlike any she'd ever known. More than once, she feared for their lives as they inched their way back down the fell, slipping, sliding, bruising, and barely able to see.

Despite the treacherous terrain, she managed to keep hold of the bag of bilberries in one hand and Lilac in the other. Once safely home, the berries were dried and stored.

As Grace reflected on the bilberries and the storm, she set to work. Although it would be some time before the soap would be ready for either of them to use, the intention would be in place and that was one of the most important aspects.

Grace reached into the Irish pine dresser and took out the large jar of dried bilberries. She left some whole for decoration purposes, and ground the rest down into powder. Before continuing with the soapmaking, she decided to sprinkle some bilberry dust at the threshold of the doorway to ward off negative energies. Whatever cloud had darkened her doorstep, she wanted it gone. Banished with the wind.

And so the conjuring began: oils, colours, scents, and then the bog bilberry. As she stirred the mixture by hand, adding the final flourishes, she knew the recipe wouldn't be complete until she added her invocation. How could she possibly make soaps in the ways of her foremothers if she didn't call in the energies? It would be another few hours until Caleb left for the day, and she couldn't wait that long.

Would Caleb conclude that she was more than a soapmaker? There was nothing for it, she had to work quickly! She couldn't send him out, or on an errand. If he was witness to the soap which would help them both, then maybe that wasn't a bad thing?

Grace closed her eyes, breathed in deeply, settled her energy, and then invoked the spirit of the bilberry to guide and guard the users of the soap. Clear in her intention, she spoke calmly.

"Bilberry of the bog,
from the strength of the Cumbrian countryside,
once rooted in Mother Earth,
berries of distilled sunshine,
strong and secure in storms,
bring forth your resilience.

Layer yourself into this soap to bring protection.
No matter where lightning strikes,
protect home and heart,
happiness and hearth."

Not once did she look Caleb's way. Not for a second did she acknowledge his presence in the room. And nor did she flinch at her craft being exposed in front of a stranger.

Afterwards, Grace poured the mix into loaves and then placed them all on the most recently made curing rack. "This rack is great," she said, admiring it as she placed each loaf there. "Six weeks from now, and my first soaps from the Cumbrian Collection will be ready," she said, pleased with the violet-coloured hue of the soap.

"Just in time for the Autumn storms," he said, knowingly.

Peace settled between them.

For now.

Bilberry Soap

We began life long before this day. As berries, we appear in the Summer and early Autumn. Many people walking the fells gather us for jams and other preserves. Indeed, we've been used in traditional medicine for over a thousand years to treat diabetes and disorders of the gastrointestinal tract.

We felt her joy, that day, and the delight of being up on the moors in high Summer. And each of us called out to her hoping to be heard; destined for her hands. Mostly she was absorbed with the way the gentle breeze invigorated her, and the vistas as far as the eye could see. Nearby, she was gathering purple-flowering heather, sphagnum moss, and other local plants, as the cadences of the skylark above invited her towards us. We sensed her reverence for every living thing, and that's how we knew: how we knew that she would find us. Invisible threads across time and space, kindred spirits connected across the plant and human realms. We sang, and she listened.

As she held us in her hands, we felt cradled: loved, valued, recognised. Many, many times that morning, we heard her whisper "Thank you. Thank you for finding me."

For hours she wandered amongst the hollows and hummocks around us, before driving rain forced her back down the pathless moorland, through bogs, knolls, farmland, and tracks by the river's edge.

Now we are preparing for the purpose of our lifetime: *to protect from the storm*. We did it for her once before, and we can do it again.

Recipes and Resources

As Grace updated the blog at dragonflysoaps.com, she described the recipes and resources of her work. To her great surprise, she'd really grown to love blogging, and sharing her craft with others as well as offering a window to 'Meet the Maker'.

Always careful, though, not to share a photo of her face lest her true identity be discovered, she provided ample photos of her studio, the soapmaking process, her hands, the flowers in her garden, and so on. Generous with her knowledge and experience, she'd garnered quite a following of soapmakers as well as those who'd never made soap but simply because they were enchanted by her love of the plant world.

Don't rush the process, she wrote. When creating a recipe, consider all the elements. It's not just about what scents might work well together, but what is the purpose: is the soap to lather? To slough? To clean? To beautify? To moisturise?

When I make soap, I ask: what do I want to put out in the world?

Soapmaking is no different to the rest of life, not really. We learn what works, what doesn't work. And we seek out those who can best help us with this creative process.

Our life is art, too, and those we surround ourselves with should be cheerleaders, silent or otherwise, but there beside us on the journey.

Soap for Madge

"I've been thinking, Caleb, that you should take some soap just for Madge. I know I've given you a few bars, but she needs her own soap. Something special."

"Why?" he asked, somewhat suspiciously.

"Why not? Every woman deserves to be pampered."

"Madge uses unscented soap. Always has. Always will."

"Why?"

"Why not?" he answered.

"Okay, you got me. I just thought it might be a nice thing to do. Come and take a look in my store cupboards and choose one for her."

Grace led the way to the oak merchant's drawers and said "Take your pick!"

Sensing his reluctance, she laughed: "It's just soap, Caleb. There's nothing to be scared of!"

"Actually, your soap scares me very much, Grace! Truth of the matter is I think you scare me too. Your soap is…"

"My soap is what?" she asked.

"Your soap has a life of its own. You can't deny it. If I didn't know better, I'd think they were living creatures! Seriously, depending which one I use, I feel completely different that day. What exactly is it that they do to people, Grace?"

"It's soap, Caleb! Now, come and choose."

Caleb starting reading out the labels:

"Juniper and Lime," he said.

"Juniper for evergreen love, and lime for fidelity," she replied.

"Rose and patchouli," he said, placing it to one side as a possibility.

"Rose is for love and patchouli works to heal any feelings of isolation or separation," she said encouragingly, and was surprised that he immediately put it back with the other soaps.

He read through the labels on several others:

"Lemongrass and Ginger; Lemon and lavender. Ylang ylang; Rose and blackcurrant; Black fig and honey; Coconut and cranberry; Clove and pineapple."

"Enhances love and sexual feelings," she said of the last soap.

Caleb looked at Grace, raised his eyebrows, and then placed the soap back down as a no go.

"Soap speaks a language. And if you listen, you'll hear it."

"I knew it! You *do* do something!"

"What about one of these?" she asked, ignoring the accusation. "Jasmine and sandalwood? Strawberry and saffron? Gardenia? Chocolate and Citrus? Charcoal, Cedarwood and Tea tree?"

"What would you choose, Grace?"

"Do you mean for me or for Madge?"

"Madge. What does she *'need'*?" he said, finally acknowledging to himself that each soap was set with a specific intention.

"Peppermint, Eucalyptus and Kelp. To be centred in one's spirituality. Clears away negative energy."

She stopped there, and omitted to add the kelp was to help those stuck and unable to leave tangled relationships.

"Or there's rose geranium or Winter spice," she suggested. She knew better than to interfere in their relationship but it was just so hard to stand back when they weren't right for each other. Reluctantly, she took the peppermint soap from his hands and said "Here, give her this one."

"Rose and blackcurrant?" he said, taking it from her, standing far too close for either of them to feel comfortable. "And what does this one mean?"

Grace looked to the floor, realising that he saw her for who she was: a magic maker, and truth be told, a script disruptor. There was no hiding from him. He might not have been able to fully articulate just what it was she crafted in this studio but he did know that it was more than soap.

"Blackcurrant is linked to the throat chakra, the place in our body where we find expression. Should Madge choose to use this soap it will clear any blockages in that part of her aura."

"And?" he asked.

"Allow her to speak her truth."

"And?" he asked again.

"What?"

"Tell me everything so I know what to expect, Grace."

"Hopefully it will bring calm to the home and to shield her from any negativity in her life…"

"You mean protect her from *me*?" he said, feeling hurt. "You think I'm the cause of her problems?"

"No, not at all. You asked for my opinion, and my opinion is that she needs to speak her truth. I don't think she's ever truly done that, not to you and not to anyone."

"Grace, Madge is the most direct, blunt and caustic person you could ever meet! I doubt she has any problem saying what's on her mind. I've spent my whole marriage having to apologise for her because she's always upsetting one person or another. Speaking the truth isn't her issue!"

"There's a world of difference between what you're describing and someone sharing their vulnerabilities, Caleb. Look, the last thing that I want to do is get in the middle of your marriage. Honestly. But…"

"But what, Grace?" he said, verging on impatience.

"You're not happy, Caleb. I sensed that the first day I met you. And that was long before I started getting to know you. If you're not happy, then the truth is that she's not happy either."

"All relationships have ups and downs, Grace. That's the reality."

"Maybe. Maybe not. I don't know. But I do know that life's too short for you to stay in this state of maintenance. It's killing both of you."

"What am I supposed to do? I made vows for life. Believe it or not, I take those seriously. I can't just change my mind because I don't have any feelings for her! We have a child. We have a life together!"

"Yes, but is that what you want?"

Sour Suds

When Caleb arrived home from work that night, the last thing he expected to see was Chell sitting on the sofa with a suitcase beside her.

"Caleb," she spoke softly. "Thank you so much for letting me move in. Madge said you were all on board. Thank you."

All at once he felt his heart sink; not only was he in for sleeping on a lumpy sofa night after night for god knows how long, and not having any respite from Ciara and Arthur, but he now had no opportunity to talk to Madge about their marriage. It had been a subject he'd studiously avoided for so long. Grace was right. It needed to be confronted.

"Of course it's fine, Chell. I hope you're happier here, and that you feel safer and cared for. Madge will be pleased to have you under our roof."

"I really can stay on the sofa. There's no need for you to give up your side of the bed."

"Not at all. It's no hardship," he said, touching her gently on the shoulder. "Now, cup of tea?"

"Yes, please."

After he switched on the kettle, he set out two mugs then headed upstairs to see Madge.

"I've brought you something," he said, passing over the soap to Madge. "I haven't been entirely honest with you. The soap is handmade, and is made by a client. I didn't want you to feel uncomfortable so I said it was from the garden centre. Here. This is for you."

"The environmental madwoman?" Madge said, cuttingly, wanting confirmation even though she knew the truth.

"That's not how I'd describe her. Nature lover. Astute business woman. Creative entrepreneur. Yes. Here. Take it. It's blackcurrant soap. I hope you like it."

"I know you've been at her house. I saw your truck there. Why didn't you tell me you were working for her?"

"You're spying on me?" he sighed. "Because you and I hardly talk these days, Madge. Because…because I didn't want you reading anything into it. She needed a carpenter for her soapmaking studio. I'm making her soap racks. End of."

"Why would I read anything into it?" she asked.

"The way you reacted about the soap made me feel inclined not to say anything."

"I wish you had said something. I don't trust you. I don't trust you at all. How much longer will you be working there?"

"Maybe another few weeks, on and off. I'm not sure."

"I don't want you to go back, Caleb. Not tomorrow. Not any day. For the sake of our marriage, if you have any love left for me at all, don't go back. I forbid you!"

"It's my work, Madge! How do you expect me to keep a roof over our head if I don't take work when it's offered to me?"

When Madge showered that night, just before bed, she couldn't decide whether to try the soap she'd bought from the garden centre or the one Caleb had brought home. *Blackcurrant and rose*, she murmured, taking the bar into her hands and allowing the lather to build up under the spray of the shower. Blackcurrant. Like mid

Summer. Addictive and pleasant. Madge felt herself lighten as frustrations washed down the plughole, and as she reflected on his confession, she wondered if she should give him advance warning that she'd told the elders he'd been alone with a woman. A non-Jehovah's Witness woman. Yes, it was time to tell him the truth.

Layers, Stripes and Swirls

The art of making beautiful soap is about layers, stripes, swirls, colours, scents, oils, and a hint of magic, **Grace** wrote on her blog.

It's no different to life, really, she reflected as she watched Caleb on the far side of the studio measuring lengths of dowel. He'd been quiet today, and she sensed he was impatient to be finished with her as a client. By insisting he take soap for Madge, she'd clearly overstepped the mark. It wasn't the right time to ask if she liked it, so she carried on writing her blog, trying to stay focused on the task at hand.

We build layers in our lives: kindness, care, generosity, humour… And then there are the stripes of remembrance and passion, and swirls of empathy.

Life is complex, and yet if you really look at it, it's all so simple: we make choices, and each choice we make moves us further along the path of life. We are the creators of our own Destiny. Soap teaches us to wash away anything that doesn't belong to us.

Lilac and Loneliness

When the school holidays arrived, Lilac joyfully threw her schoolbag across the kitchen floor. "I can't wait to play all day long, every day", she squealed excitedly. Grace knew Summer holidays meant a constant juggle between maintaining the business and being a mother all hours of the day. As with previous years, they found a reliable rhythm between each other's needs and desires. Lilac often headed into the garden to play, coming inside only when her belly growled with hunger.

Caleb was sanding down the frame of a soap rack when he saw Lilac standing beneath the canopy of an old oak tree with her cheek pressed to the trunk.

"Grace?" he said, turning towards her, "You know, I have plenty of unused pieces of timber at home in my shed. I could make her a tree house, if you like? That tree is just begging for something like that."

Grace closed the lid of her laptop and walked to the edge of the conservatory. Without saying a word, she stepped outside and joined Lilac, then placed her palms upon the trunk. Although Caleb couldn't hear what she was saying, he sensed she was speaking to the tree. It wouldn't have surprised him if she was asking it for permission. From the smile on Lilac's face, he figured he was right. Lilac stretched her arms around the tree trunk, and then around Grace's waist.

Grace smiled as she came back indoors.

"Sounds like a wonderful idea, Caleb. Send me an invoice, and then fit it in as and when you can. Thank you so much. Lilac and her dollies will love it!"

"There'll be no invoice, Grace. It's a gift. It's the

least I can do. Being here has changed my life."

"Changed your life? How?"

"You've opened a door. Watching you, and how you've adapted to this whole new life in a place that's not your own, has made me think. I've been questioning things for a long time, especially about how out of place I am in my own life. I'm caught. I've been stuck for so long between choosing my family or choosing freedom. Just by living your life I'm starting to see what I can reclaim for myself. The treehouse is a gift. A place for Lilac to play."

"That's so kind; so generous and thoughtful, Caleb. Really."

With each passing day, she felt herself growing closer to Caleb, and each evening as he left to go home to his family, she resolved to be strong and solid within herself: NO.

When Grace said she was heading off to the kitchen to heat some lunch, Caleb stopped work and joined Lilac in the garden.

"Mummy asked the tree if you could build me a treehouse. Thank you, Caleb!" she said, hugging him tight.

They sat, side by side, on the grass by the base of the tree talking about flowers, bees, and the clouds in the sky.

Lilac sighed. "I miss my grandmother. Mummy says that we'll meet again one day, but I don't know when that will be. She lives on the other side of the world. Do you think she'll come here one day?" she asked, but didn't wait for an answer. "I miss my preschool friends, too. I think about them, you know? Every day. I have new friends now, but I still miss my old ones. I miss a lot of things about home."

"This is your home now," Caleb said gently.

"I know. That's what Mummy tells me every day, but I don't know it. I don't know the flowers very well and the sunshine is different here. Even the breeze feels different on my skin. Like a stranger."

Caleb had a thought. "Maybe you need to make friends with the breeze."

"Make friends?" she giggled, as if it were a silly idea.

"Wait here," Caleb said, and jogged to his pick-up truck. There, inside the glovebox, he pulled out a small bag.

When he returned to Lilac, he opened it and said "This is a pocket-sized kite. Shall we fly it?"

Lilac jumped to her feet.

"Come on, Lilac, let's go make friends with the breeze."

For Caleb, it felt like the most natural thing in the world to help Lilac lift that kite up on the invisible energies of the wind and watch it go higher and higher. For a moment, he imagined it was him flying away from all that had restrained him across the years of his life. Away from indoctrination, and toxic ideologies, free and untethered. If only. If only he could just slip away, with no fuss, no public shaming, and begin life anew.

"Lunch is ready," Grace called through the door, her words finding them at the end of the rambling garden. "That looks fun!"

"Oh Mummy, Mummy. We had the best time! I made friends with the breeze. I know it now. I really, really know it!"

"I think the breeze knows you too, Lilac," Caleb said.

"Can we eat outside, Mummy?"

"Sure, I'll bring it out."

They settled on a picnic blanket, garlanded by the beautiful borders of the blue starflowers and pink cosmos blossoms slowly swaying in the breeze.

"This tastes so good," Caleb said, eating the red pepper and feta quiche. "So good!"

Summertime settled around them bringing the promise of hope, adventure and friendship. Afterwards, Grace said "You two enjoy this sunshine a bit longer before Caleb gets back to work. I'll just run these plates inside."

When the phone call came, Caleb was telling Lilac the story of when he was a boy and ended up lost.

When the phone call came, Caleb saw his life disappearing as if down a plug hole. Swallowed whole. For several moments, he could hardly breathe.

When the phone call came, it was bittersweet: a door both closing and opening. Shock and relief. A way out?

"Caleb, please come in and see us for a meeting," Stan said. "Tonight, please. 7pm. We'll be waiting for you."

It was like a schoolboy being called up before the headmaster, but somehow so much worse. His whole life hung in the balance: all he knew rested within the circle of the Jehovah's Witness community. Not only had he forfeited a university education and taken the consolation prize of pursuing an apprenticeship, but friendships he'd yearned to forge were discouraged, as was his keen interest in joining a rock band. "Too worldly," he was warned, over and over again. And so, instead, he married young, became a father long before he was ready, and devoted himself to the community, holding Bible study classes and pioneering, actively involved in the door-to-door ministry.

Many, many times, he wondered how different his life would have been had his father chosen not to indoctrinate Caleb and his siblings in the faith.

At seven sharp, he pulled up into the carpark of the Kingdom Hall. Two other cars were in the otherwise vacant lot. With an abrupt tug at his tie, he wondered what he would say? What would they ask? Surely it wasn't a sin to be doing carpentry at Grace's house? It's not like he needed chaperoning! They weren't involved. And they certainly weren't dating or in a relationship.

The meeting was formal and straight to the point.

"Caleb, we're concerned. Not only have you been unshaven more often than not, we've noticed you're not singing during meetings, and failing to attend regularly. When was the last time you went door knocking or out on the trolleys?"

"I'm working. I'm working long hours. I've got a family to provide for and it's near impossible to do it on one income, let alone a part-time income."

"Jehovah must come first, Caleb."

"Jehovah isn't going to pay my rent!" he yelled, uncharacteristically.

"Caleb."

"Madge doesn't work. The responsibility lies with me. I have a teenage daughter who needs clothes, shoes, makeup, school books. Where's Jehovah? It's not like he's miraculously putting funds into my bank account."

"Caleb it has been brought to our attention that

you've been keeping company with a young lady from outside our community."

"She's a client. I'm doing carpentry and cabinet making for her."

"Madge is concerned. She fears…"

"Madge is wrong! She's way out of line. Nothing's happened. Nothing at all."

"Are you attracted to this woman?" Noel asked him.

Caleb fell silent. How could he answer that?

"Caleb?"

"What do you mean am I *attracted* to her?"

"It's a simple question. Are you attracted to her? Do you feel aroused when you're with her? Are you having a sexual relationship with this woman?"

"Don't be ridiculous. Of course not! I'm married. There has been zero physical intimacy between us. Grace is a lovely woman. I find her kindness attractive but that doesn't mean anything other than that she's a nice person!"

"So you do find her attractive?"

"Yes!" he said, exasperated.

"Caleb we are going to instruct you to stop working there. This situation can't go on. Caleb, you must cease all engagement with that woman. You know that we don't encourage worldly activities like spending any length of time with those who are not part of our community."

"I'm working there. I haven't finished my contract."

"This woman will have to find another carpenter. As your spiritual supporters, we are advising that you don't see her again."

"No," Caleb said, wondering for a moment if

he'd used Madge's blackcurrant soap. He found the word came to him easily. "No, I'm not going to do as you ask. I'm an adult. A grown man. I'm simply going about my business."

"You leave us no choice, Caleb. We'll have to take disciplinary action against you. One last time: Will you stop seeing her?"

"No."

"Is that your final answer?

Caleb didn't respond but simply left the room.

If he'd had an affair and cheated on Madge, he could have understood their hard line. But to be admonished simply for being in the same room as her without another adult around was incomprehensible. And yet, if he was honest, as an elder there'd been many occasions when he'd had to speak to a brother or sister in the congregation about spending time with a non Jehovah's Witness.

The drive home that night was long and slow. Home was the last place he wanted to go. Another evening on the sofa, another evening listening to Chell talk about Jehovah. One more night of Ciara and Arthur cuddling on the sofa. Another evening of... What? Emptiness? Another evening of his life wasted? Another day he'd never get back again?

Was there anything good in his life anymore? It seemed the only joy he'd had in recent times was whenever he was with Grace. Grace and Lilac.

As he tossed and turned on the sofa all night, Caleb wondered what lay ahead. Whatever way he looked at it, his connection with Grace would soon be ending. The treehouse would be built in his spare time. He could hardly just pop by and visit her. And now the elders had spoken, he wondered what action they'd take. It was the longest and loneliest night of his life.

View From the Treehouse

Each evening after a long day of work, Caleb's focus was on building Lilac the best treehouse possible. It only took a couple of weeks, however it meant skipping every meeting at the Kingdom Hall and enduring the inevitable earful from Madge each time he arrived home late.

There was immense joy to be found in watching Lilac's face light up at each stage of the process: digging in and placing the supporting posts, the laying of solid flooring, erecting a safe set of stairs, the building of walls, fashioning windows with love-heart shutters, putting a slate roof in place, and finally a verandah with railings. Even before he'd hammered in the last nails or completed a thorough safety check, Lilac was busy transporting dolls and baskets of soap up the steps—quicker and quieter than a new mother cat moves a litter of kittens—and into the treehouse making herself right at home.

When Caleb first suggested the idea of creating a cubby for Lilac, a simple outside space for play, his thoughts never went as far as her own motivation for what this treehouse would mean: it was hers, a safe space with a view, where she belonged and could adapt at will, and in doing so, bloom as brightly as the blossoms below.

He listened intently to her magic making as she imitated the incantations she'd heard Grace speak in the studio.

"This soap is for love," she said, placing it to one side. "One day they'll kiss and get married. And this soap means a visitor is coming."

When Caleb placed his tools to one side and removed a few pieces of unused wood from the floor, he turned to Lilac and said "Sorry to disturb you in your work, but do you fancy giving your Mum the grand tour?"

"In a minute, Caleb. I'm just making a spell. Shhhh."

A woman's work is never done. He smiled, and then swept up some sawdust.

The garden couldn't have looked prettier, here in the height of Summer. The view from the treehouse meant that Lilac could see right across the rambling garden, up to the meadows and fells, as well as into the soapmaking studio always secure in the knowledge that her mother was visible and nearby.

As she tinkered and talked, speaking spells and separating out her soaps, Caleb went to his truck and fetched a little housewarming gift for Lilac. He returned with some fairylights, and when there was a moment of silence, he asked "Lilac, would you like these fairylights in here?"

Caleb flicked on the switch, and watched her eyes shine at the subtle amber tones coming from each tiny star. "Thank you!" she exclaimed, hugging him tightly.

"Where would you like them?"

Lilac surveyed the room, and then instructed Caleb to drape them around a window frame, and the doorway.

"Excellent choice, Lilac."

Caleb pinned them up, and stapled them around the frames.

"Looks perfect," he said.

Lilac padded around the beautifully sanded

floorboards, and then spread out a small pink rug she'd poached from her bedroom.

"Okay, you can call Mummy now," Lilac said a few minutes later when she felt everything was complete.

When she saw Grace follow Caleb into the garden, Lilac looked down proudly from her vantage point and beamed.

"Look Mummy, it has a verandah with rails so I don't fall down, and windows so I can see you in the studio. There's a table inside and chairs. And a roof. Isn't it just the best house in the whole world? Caleb did all this for me!"

"You're a lucky girl, Lilac. We're both lucky to have Caleb here. Can I come up?"

"It's strong enough for adults," Caleb assured her.

Caleb lay down on the grass listening to them chatter about this and that, and what soap worked best for what, and Lilac told Grace how if you listen you can hear the leaves of the oak tree whisper in the wind.

He couldn't help smile when he heard Lilac's enthusiasm about the design.

"And feel the bark, Mummy. Isn't Caleb clever the way he built this house around the tree?"

"Clever Caleb," Grace agreed.

"Mummy?"

"Yes, love?"

"Let's have dinner up here tonight. My new home needs a celebration. You always say that sitting around the table makes a house feel welcoming and more like a home. That's what this home needs."

"Okay. Do you think we'll all fit up here?"

"Yes!" came Caleb's voice through the floorboards. "It was built for the three of us to eat in there. I'll go grab the dinner from the kitchen. You stay there."

After Lilac was tucked into bed that night, Caleb got ready to leave. "I had the best night tonight, Grace. It's just so easy being here. And it's always so hard going home."

"Caleb, you know the grass is always greener where we water it. Of course it's easy being here. All your attention is here, you work here, you eat here, you play with Lilac here. You've built her the best treehouse ever. It's only natural that you feel at home. I'm glad you do. But...if you want to make your marriage work, then you have to focus on your family and not mine," she said reluctantly.

"That's easier said than done, Grace. It's a lot more natural to put your energy into people and places where you're welcomed, and where you feel valued and appreciated."

"Are you at least going to try?" she asked. "Give Madge and your marriage a chance?"

The Bug

"What's wrong, Grace?" Caleb asked just as he was getting ready to leave at the end of the work day.

"I don't feel so good," she said, head in her hands as she leaned over the workbench.

"Let me take a look at you," he said, feeling her forehead. "Feels like you've got a temperature. How long have you felt like this?"

"It just came on, about half an hour ago."

They were interrupted by Lilac coming in, crying.

"What's wrong, sweetheart?" Grace asked.

"I just vomited all over my bed; there's sick everywhere," Lilac cried, cuddling into her mother.

"Sound like a bug," Caleb said. "I'll come and clean it up, and get you both to bed. Come on, Grace, you too."

Caleb led the way, and set to removing the bedding in Lilac's room, and replacing it with fresh linen. Lilac sat on the armchair in her room watching him tend to the space. In a short while, he'd found Grace's cleaning supplies and used a mix of tea-tree and eucalyptus oil to disinfect and freshen the room, and then brought in a large stainless-steel bowl in case Lilac was sick again.

As he settled the little girl back into bed, Lilac asked Caleb to tell her a story. Just when he started, he heard Grace rush to the bathroom. It was in that moment, that he realised he wouldn't be going home anytime soon. Grace needed him. They both needed him.

From time to time, for the next couple of hours, Caleb alternated from one bedroom to the other, checking on Grace and Lilac, and ensuring they stayed hydrated.

In two minds as to whether he should inform Madge of his whereabouts, he sent a simple text:

Home late.
Don't wait up.

Caleb found a couple of magazines in the living room, brewed a pot of tea and snaffled a cookie from the kitchen, then read long, long into the night. He made himself comfortable in the deep armchair of Lilac's bedroom, and wondered how often Grace had sat on the chair waiting for Lilac to fall asleep. Somehow it had the word 'patience' written all over it.

The bedroom was simply decorated, in shades of lilac, with floral curtains and soft carpet. In one corner, was a reading nook: a tipi with cushions and blankets, and in the other a dressing table and mirror with the words "Lilac is beautiful" stencilled onto the mirror.

From time to time his reading was punctuated by the sounds of Lilac crying and being sick, and Grace scrambling out of bed and rushing to the toilet. Each time, he'd get up from the armchair and sit by their side waiting until the latest evacuation was over and they were settled again.

"Would you rather I brought you a bowl or bucket into your bedroom?" Caleb asked Grace, bringing her a cool flannel, and refilling her glass.

"No," she said, "but thanks. I'm fine. I'm just so tired." Grace looked at her bedside clock. "It's 4am! What are you still doing here?"

"I'm not going anywhere while you're both so poorly. Get some sleep," he said, tucking the duvet around her. "Sleep."

When Caleb headed back to the living room to look for some more magazines, he was sure he saw a small light in the driveway. *What is that? Where's it coming from?*

Curious, he quietly left the house and walked up the path. And there, at the end of the driveway beneath a sycamore tree, was a car he knew well. If it wasn't for the light of a mobile phone, he might never have known they were there. Max and Stewart, two elders from the congregation, sat down low in their seats so Caleb wouldn't see them.

"What are you two doing here?" Caleb asked, opening the driver's door.

"Madge told us you hadn't come home last night."

"And? What are you? Spiritual policemen? This is ridiculous!"

"Caleb, you've already been warned, and you've admitted that you have feelings for this woman. And now you're here all night long? What are we to think? Two of us have witnessed this. You know what this will mean for you now, don't you?"

"Grace is sick. Lilac is sick. They've been vomiting all night. I'm here helping them, not having sex!"

"Caleb, do you really expect us to believe that?"

Alpine Forget-Me-Not

Lilac played in the garden, in view of Grace. It was the last day of Caleb working in the studio. The air felt heavy, and neither of them said a word. Not in the mood or right frame of mind for soapmaking, Grace packed up all the new orders which had come in during the week. As she pottered about the studio, singing along to Taylor Swift's *Best Day*, she looked over to Caleb wondering what was going through his mind. She sensed his sadness, almost as if it were her own, but felt like it was far deeper than the fact they'd be parting ways today. For a while she tried making smalltalk to see if he'd smile or engage in any meaningful way. When that failed, she carried on sorting soaps into categories.

"May I give you one last soap?" Grace asked, as the afternoon neared its end and Caleb packed up his tools ready to leave.

"I'm not sure that's a good idea," he said, half smiling. "Your soaps haven't exactly helped my life!"

"Caleb, the soaps I make are for hope and healing. They don't have the power to ruin your life."

"I wouldn't be too sure of that," he said, packing up his tools.

"This is Alpine Forget-Me-Not."

"It's a pretty colour, I'll give you that. You're a talented and creative woman."

"This flower is for fidelity, faithfulness, and a promise to always remember."

"I don't understand. I haven't been unfaithful to anyone. Grace, you know that!"

"Maybe it's about being faithful to yourself,

Caleb? I don't know why I'm drawn to give you this soap but I hope you'll accept it with the spirit in which it is given."

"I will always remember you, Grace. Thank you for brightening my life."

"You've brightened mine, too, Caleb. Never forget that." She spontaneously reached forward and hugged him, surprising them both. Lilac came rushing indoors and joined the hug.

"Please come back and visit," the little girl pleaded. "I like having you here. It's like you belong."

"You're so kind, Lilac. I sure am going to miss you. And your Mum."

"Then you must come back! I'll cast a spell on you!" Lilac said, lifting up the long-stemmed yellow rosebud she'd been playing with, and pointing it at him.

"Ah, like mother like daughter, hey?"

"You could say that," Grace laughed. "Thank you for everything. I'm so grateful. Be kind to yourself, Caleb. Go well."

It was all she could do to hold back the tears, and she wondered if he felt it too.

The Shunning Begins

Caleb hadn't planned to go to the meeting at the Kingdom Hall that evening. His gut told him to stay home and read a book instead.

"You haven't been for five weeks, Caleb," Madge said for the fourth time in half an hour. Not wanting Chell to witness any more discord he simply said "Okay. I'll go."

"Why do you make it sound like such a hardship, Caleb? Just get dressed and hurry up!"

"Come on, Dad. You're holding us all up," Ciara said, texting at the same time.

As he dressed in his suit and tie, the scent of soap lured him to the bathroom. There were soaps Madge had bought, and the gifts he'd received from Grace. How simple her world seemed: and how he missed his days with her and Lilac. The peace. The laughter. The ease.

"Caleb! Hurry up!"

He sighed, then walked down the stairs and helped Chell to the car.

"Are you sure you're up to going, Chell?" he asked with tenderness. "I can stay home with you," he offered.

"No, Caleb," Madge said, her voice low and growl-like. "No. You need to go to meetings regularly, and to get back to Bible studies. It's ridiculous that you're working all the time, or too tired to go out on the ministry. What's wrong with you?"

As they took their seats in the Kingdom Hall that night, Caleb sat quietly and studied his hands; hands which had crafted curing racks for Grace, and built a beautiful treehouse for Lilac. Hands which taught that little girl how to fly a kite and know the wind as a friend. Hands which reached out to Grace every time she brewed him a coffee. Hands which longed to hold her in his arms.

That night, he barely heard the words being spoken until an elder stood up to speak about excommunications.

"Caleb Alden is no longer a Jehovah's Witness." Hearing his name jolted him back into the room. Although Caleb knew that about 60,000 witnesses around the world are disfellowshipped each year, somehow hearing his name felt like his head being on the executioner's block. Everything in his life was about to change.

The elder didn't say why he was expelled. Witnesses would make their own assumptions: smoking, slander, violence, apostasy, anger, intercourse with someone of the same gender, fraud, drunkenness, fornication, gambling or adultery. And although he knew that he wasn't guilty of any of them, not a single one, he also knew what it meant, and what those in this congregation had to do: shun Caleb. If they didn't, they'd also risk being disfellowshipped; to protect themselves from this 'unrepentant wrongdoer', and protect the congregation from moral and spiritual contamination.

Caleb knew better than anyone what was about to happen: by supporting the decision, the witnesses would hope to influence his heart, as a person who has done wrong, and in doing so encourage him to come to his senses, and return to Jehovah. As his life flashed before his eyes, he thought of all the times he'd been obligated to disfellowship a member. Amongst witnesses, it's considered the highest form of discipline.

Would he die at Armageddon? After all, this is what he'd been indoctrinated with his whole life. And now, he was left wondering. Was an eternity in Armageddon really the price he had to pay for refusing to stop working with Grace?

From this day forward, his friends and family would have to shun him. Caleb braced himself. As he left the Kingdom Hall that night, there were no goodbyes, no eye contact. Not a single friend acknowledged his presence. The public shaming had begun.

If only he had someone to talk to. But everyone he knew was now under strict instructions to have no contact with him until he came to his senses. As he drove Madge, Chell and Ciara home, it occurred to Caleb that he rather enjoyed the silence in the car that night.

Home Sour Home

Day after day, it was like he was invisible. Caleb filled a cafetiere with coffee and asked Madge if she'd like some. No eye contact, no acknowledgement. In response, she pulled open the cupboard, grabbed a mug, and made herself instant coffee.

His mother-in-law, Chell, who'd always been so kind and friendly and had now spent weeks sleeping on his side of the bed, didn't look at him at all.

For the sake of peace, Caleb knew there was only one way to end this: to go to the elders and repent. Repent for what, exactly? Doing his job as a carpenter? For not cancelling his work with Grace when they'd insisted?

Caught in the ideology of something he no longer felt part of, each day was like living in solitary confinement. Rather than go stir crazy, it somehow strengthened his resolve. Why was he the only one who could see how ludicrous this was?

After breakfast, Caleb went through his invoices. Some clients were slow to pay. Again. It was one thing to shun him, but a whole different matter to hold back on payments. How much longer could he sustain his family and keep a roof over their heads? For all these years he'd managed to successfully run his own business. Self-employed life often had its financial ups and downs, but this was the most fallow time he'd ever experienced. *Should I go out and find a new job?*

"We need to tighten our belts, Madge," he said softly while she was reading a Watchtower magazine. "Money is short. I need your help if we're going to stay afloat."

Not once did she look up and acknowledge his words.

"Madge. This is serious. Please. Even if you don't want to talk to me, will you at least listen to what I have to say? We're in our overdraft, and that's mostly used up. There's nowhere else we can go, financially. I need you to stop spending so much money at the supermarket and buying clothes for Ciara every time you're out. I've no idea why our expenses have gone through the roof. Please. At least for a while until things pick up."

When she didn't reply he said, "The other option is that you go out and get a job."

At her lack of response, Caleb stood up and said "The third option is that I leave. For good."

Autumn

`Hi Caleb,` Grace texted on the spur of the moment, a couple of months after his last day working at her place.

`I know this seems a bit out of the blue, but Lilac and I were just wondering how you are. No need to reply if it doesn't feel right, but just wanted you to know we're thinking about you. Grace.`

After she hit send, she sent another text.

`We miss you. G & L xx`

Grace hit 'send' before she had time to change her mind. Although theirs had been a professional relationship, they both knew their deep conversations about being out of place in this world had bonded them, and within each other's company they had found a place to settle: the forging of a friendship. And then she wondered why they hadn't stayed in touch.

When Caleb received the text notification, Ciara was stomping around the kitchen yelling at Madge. "It's so selfish for Dad to go and get himself disfellowshipped. So selfish, I tell ya! I hardly get to spend any time with Arthur now because there's no one to chaperone us. You're always out on Bible study or out door-knocking. It's not fair! Just not fair! I don't even have a life anymore. Dad! Dad? Can't you just repent so we can go back to normal?"

Caleb looked up at his daughter, so youthful, vulnerable and innocent and yet at the cusp of adulthood, and then quietly walked upstairs to read the message.

Grace's words were a balm: a ray of light brightening up his dark world. It was the first friendly contact he'd had with anyone since he last saw her. Most of his carpentry projects were for brothers and sisters in his religious community, and almost all of them were cancelled since the day of the disfellowshipping. There was enough work from a local bakery to help make ends meet, but financial resources had dwindled to almost nothing. With Chell living in the house, there were added expenses there, too. For the next half hour, he kept rereading the texts. What would he say? How could he tell her that just knowing she was thinking of him meant more than she could ever know?

```
Dear Grace and Lilac
Not a single day goes by where I
don't think about you, and your
lovely life at Dragonfly Cottage.
It's fair to say that my time there
was the best Summer of my life. I
can't thank you enough for that.
```

He typed the message, erased it, retyped it, erased it, and retyped it, before adding:
```
I miss both of you too, and I hope
that our paths cross again. Sooner
rather than later, would be nice.
Caleb xx
```

Realising that it would be good to find a reason to meet, he quickly followed it up with another text:

```
I don't suppose the bilberry soap is
ready? The storm sure is wild. I've
battened down the hatches, but it's
not enough.
```

Caleb wondered if he should explain, or if Grace would sense there were dark days afoot. No matter which way he turned, the storm was dismantling anything solid in his life. For the next hour he lay on his bed waiting for a reply, but when there was none he wondered if he'd said too much. Should he have simply responded with 'nice to hear from you, hope you're both well'?

Ciara was still yelling downstairs, venting her frustrations so that even the neighbours could hear. Madge had barely said a word to Caleb since the evening he was disfellowshipped, and Ciara's pleading this evening was the first time she'd even acknowledged Caleb's existence.

This was his home, but he felt like an outcast here. If only he could escape. The house was too small for three adults, and a raging teenager.

Still no reply from Grace. Caleb decided to take a bath, a luxury he'd not enjoyed for years. It would provide a portal to peace even if just for a little while. As the tub filled, he looked for some music on his phone and listened to a jazz station, settling on Caro Emerald singing *A Night Like This.*

Caleb picked up a soap Grace had given him in a little care package. It was a 'soap on a rope' *specially formulated for men*, she said. Caleb knew with certainty that any soap Grace made was for more than cleansing.

Caleb stepped into the tub of warm water and sat down, then lay back and felt himself fully relax wondering why he rarely ever had baths. It was like another world, and a pleasant escape from the acrid atmosphere in his home.

The sweetly scented soap was crafted from fresh-cut pine, charcoal and sandalwood. Intrigued by its scent, it was almost as if he could hear Grace saying "For wisdom, transformation and renewal, and to bring you closer to the divine." *But of course she didn't say that*, he told himself. *She's not here. I'm alone.*

As he washed the length of his body, the foam from the soap yielded small bubbles that floated above the bath water. Worlds within worlds, beckoning him to a place of magic and miracles.

Caleb surveyed his body, taut and toned from years of manual work, and imagined… For just a moment. Just a moment.

Don't forget who you are, came the inner voices: *there are only two ways out of a Jehovah's Witness marriage: death or adultery*. Caleb told himself that neither of those were options. His dreams of Grace were just that: pleasant and wishful thinking. It was an impossibility to even think there was even the smallest chance of them ever being together. The reality was that Jehovah's Witnesses have about a 1% divorce rate. That night, shame bathed alongside heartbreak.

Madge was his wife, and at some point he'd succumb and seek out the elders. He'd tell them he was wrong, and slowly, uncomfortably slowly, he'd be welcomed back into the fold. And life would inevitably return to normal, whatever that was. As he thought about that, it was like walking into a dark tunnel far, far away from the luminous light of Lilac and gorgeous Grace.

Who am I? Is this what the rest of my life looks like? Conforming to other people's ideas of who I should be? Broken pieces of my past fragmented and shoved into shape?

After Grace tucked Lilac into bed that night, and sang her to sleep, she sat on the sofa ready to pick up an ecology magazine when she thought to check her phone for messages. Winds howled, and gusts rattled the old farmhouse cottage windows. It was the third named storm of the season, and she felt increasingly isolated and claustrophobic about being housebound. As she read Caleb's texts, a niggling feeling crept over her. *Is he okay?*

```
The days are certainly shorter, and
feel so much darker, don't they?
Caleb...
```

she hesitated, and then continued.

```
Would you like to come and have lunch
with Lilac and I?
```

She wondered if he'd accept the invitation, and then another thought occurred to her.

```
I know you're really busy with your
carpentry, but if you've got any
spare time, I could do with some
more curing racks being made and
storage spaces. Business is growing
rapidly, and I'd like to convert the
```

old barn. It's just a thought. Don't feel obligated. The last thing I want is to cause Madge any distress or any friction in your marriage.

It only occurred to me after you left that there's plenty of carpentry work you can do here, if you like?

I've been so focused on my soapmaking that I'd lost track of how much extra space I will need. The old barn is great. As a building, it's fantastic and is structurally sound, but it needs some work, and I need rodent-proof storage spaces for my soaps. What do you think? G xx

Rats like soap? xx he asked.

Lol xx, she replied.

A sweet sense of peace settled over them both.

Falling For Grace

Leftover Cuties were singing on the radio, *You Are My Sunshine*, and Grace and Lilac sang along exaggerating their vocals, swinging their hips, and making the most of their mock microphones in between the obligatory stirring ingredients. They'd chosen pea and halloumi fritters with charred lemon dip for their lunch with Caleb.

Grace couldn't help but think that Lilac was even more excited than she was about his impending arrival. Jazz tunes filled the kitchen competing with the drama of the Autumn storm menacing outside. Grace toasted cumin seeds in a small pan, their aroma contrasting with the lemon zest. They continued preparing lunch, setting the table, adjusting the linen placemats on the old wooden dining table, and fussing. They both wanted everything to be just right.

When the doorbell rang, Lilac squealed "He's here! He's here, Mummy! I'll let him in!"

Lilac opened the door, rescuing Caleb from the torrential downpour and beckoned him across the threshold before wrapping her arms around him.

"I've missed you so much, Caleb. We've made you lunch. Hope you're hungry." When she looked up at him, Lilac asked "Are you okay? Are you crying?"

"No, sweetheart. Just so pleased to see you."

"Mummy's in the kitchen. Come through!"

"Whatever you've made smells delicious!"

"You're going to love it, Caleb. I helped Mummy. It really is delicious." They walked, hand in hand, along the wide hallway into the old farmhouse kitchen. "Mummy, look who's here!"

"Caleb," Grace said, her voice barely above a whisper, unable to contain the fragile feeling at seeing him again all these weeks later.

Instinctively, she hugged him. Not for a moment did she second guess herself. Caleb was here as a friend, not their carpenter, and she sensed he needed that hug even more than she did. Somehow, since she saw him last, his skin wore signs of being jaded and wrung out. What had happened to make him look so withdrawn?

"You're soaked through, Caleb. Let me get a towel. Actually, come and use my hair dryer too." She beckoned him to follow, and they went into her bedroom. It occurred to him that this was completely crossing all boundaries of good behaviour as a Jehovah's Witness. But he wasn't one anymore, was he? Did it matter? There was no one he had to please or impress.

Passing him a flannelette shirt, she said "Pop this old work shirt on while we eat. It'll fit. Not fancy, I know, but it'll give me a chance to dry your top and jumper."

"Thanks, Grace," he said.

"I'll go back to the kitchen and give you some privacy." The thought of seeing him half naked was enough to make her blush.

Here, at Grace's table, Caleb let the weight of the world, of *his* world, ease away. Not that it was going to go away in a hurry, but today, for now, he was free to enjoy the company of a woman and young girl who'd so readily welcomed him into their home and hearts. Their conversation over lunch was a salve to so many savage stings of recent months.

With each passing minute, Caleb felt himself drifting softly, softly, softly into the revelation that he was falling ever so in love with Grace. There was a sweetness to be found in her company unlike anything he'd ever known before. Even if he were free to begin a relationship with her, what did he have to offer? Nothing. Absolutely nothing but a lifetime of religious baggage that he was desperately trying to unpack day after day. Life as a businessman was becoming increasingly untenable now that he was disfellowshipped. It wouldn't be long before he couldn't even pay his own way let alone provide for anyone else.

For now, though, just for the next little while, he pushed the harsh reality of life to one side and listened intently as Lilac charmed him with stories of dollies in the treehouse, and two new friends she'd made at tap-dancing class.

When the phone rang, Grace excused herself and answered it.

"Hi Fiona." She covered the mouthpiece and said to Lilac "Fiona is asking if you'd like to go ice skating with Jessica this afternoon."

As Lilac's face lit up at the possibility, she then frowned and said "What about Caleb?"

"It's fine, Lilac," he said. "You go ice skating. It sounds like fun."

"Will you come and visit us again? Will I ever see you again?" Lilac asked.

"Yes," he answered. "Yes."

"Promise?" Lilac asked, just to make sure.

"I promise."

Lilac nodded her head enthusiastically at Grace. "Yes!"

"She'll be ready for you to pick up in ten minutes, Fiona. Thanks for this. See you soon."

After a long embrace with Caleb, Lilac skipped off out the door with Fiona and Jessica for an afternoon of fun.

Grace wondered if Caleb might suddenly feel uncomfortable with just the two of them, but as they segued from lunch at the kitchen table to the comfort of the sofa in the living room, it was as if it was the most natural thing in the world. They sipped Brazilian coffee from hand-thrown pottery mugs and snaffled far too many of Grace's almond and raspberry cookies.

As she ran her hand across the armrest of the forest-green linen sofa, Grace wondered whether to shift the conversation from their favourite jazz-music singers to 'why the hell do you look so wrung out?'

As a friend, she wanted to help ease away the ghosts which lingered in his soul and haunted his eyes.

"Caleb, talk to me. What's going on? Something is very wrong, and if there's anything I can do to help you then I'd like to," she said, placing her hand on his.

"Soap," he said. "Your soap."

"My soap? What's wrong with my soap?"

"There's nothing wrong with the soap, as such, but…What is it, Grace? What is it about your soap which turns people's lives upside down?"

"You don't really believe a piece of soap can do that, do you?" she asked, alarmed at where the conversation was likely to lead.

"Grace, tell me the truth. What sort of witchcraft do you do? Should I be scared? My life is unravelling at a rate of knots, and I don't know if I should stop using any and all of the soaps you've given me, and Madge for that matter, or if…" he hesitated.

"If?" she asked, urging him on.

"If, despite everything, things are exactly as they're meant to be."

"Well, there is a truth to growth begins with chaos!" She smiled, but sensed that there was deep hurt and confusion beneath his words.

"What's going on for you, Caleb? You know there isn't anything you can't tell me."

"I don't even know where to start," he said, sighing in frustration.

"At the beginning. Or here. Or what next week might look like. Just start somewhere."

"You're the kindest person I've ever met, Grace, and while that's a lovely thing, it really is, it's also highlighting all the things and people in my life which aren't lovely. And that's confusing. I'm in turmoil. I don't know which way is up. I swear if something doesn't change in my life soon, I might end up having a breakdown. I'm at crisis point, Grace, and I honestly don't know what to do or where to go from here. I swear that sometimes the only thing that keeps me sane," he chuckled, "is when I'm in the shower or bath and using your soap! Suddenly I feel peaceful."

"And here I was thinking the soap was the cause of all your problems," she said, smiling, and then added, more seriously "When we're at crisis point, Caleb, we have a choice: breakdown or breakthrough. It *is* a choice. I can't fix things for you, but I can listen. You can tell me anything, and it won't go any further. I'm a vault like that."

"I do trust you, Grace, it's just that I don't want to burden you."

"Let me decide what's a burden. Okay?"

"I've spent my life believing Armageddon is

just around the corner. A lifetime lived in fear," he confessed.

"Rather than hope for the prophesied New World?"

"Yeah. I've felt enslaved by the ideology, and yet so indoctrinated, that the consequences of leaving the faith have kept me there. It's hard to explain it but it's like the constant coercion and manipulation transforms your identity."

"Every human being has the right to live in freedom and truth. I'll defend the right to freedom of the mind till the day I die," she said. "How can anyone feel a sense of liberation if they're enslaved by other people's ideas?"

"The language is loaded to inflict creed upon a person. You lose your authentic identity."

"You want to know how to find a way back to yourself?"

Caleb nodded.

"I have to admit, Caleb, that when we've spoken previously about life as a Jehovah's Witness I hadn't fully appreciated the depth of courage it would take for you to leave. But the truth is that if the belief system was a healthy one, you'd have the freedom to move on. It's important for any human being to challenge assumptions and to ask critical questions. Truth doesn't mind being questioned. Lies, however, do. We only get one life, Caleb. It's our birthright to choose how we wish to live."

"Sitting here with you, having this conversation, makes me an apostate. There are so many things I question, such as the governing body's policy of child rearing or their systemic failure to call the police when a child has been abused by a paedophile member.

These things aren't right, Grace."

"Of course they're wrong!"

"I wanted to leave. To quietly slip away. No fuss. Just do my own thing. I knew it wouldn't be easy. How could it be when my community of friends, my family, my whole world is part of that life?"

"I'm not part of it. I'm here, Caleb. I will always encourage you to do what you believe. To be curious, and to allow that curiosity to lead you elsewhere. Trust the magic of new beginnings and leave anything that's toxic. If my place in your life is to open your eyes to other ways of seeing the world, then I'm happy to play a part."

"I wanted to slip away quietly," he said once again. "But…I was disfellowshipped. Initially I had to present myself to the elders. They ordered me to stop working for you."

"Me? How did they even know about me?"

"Madge."

Wedding Woes

Caleb filled the kettle and set about making himself a coffee. Ciara was ranting, once again, about him being disfellowshipped and how it was ruining all her plans. Ignoring him, she spoke directly to Madge.

"Arthur wants to ask Dad permission to marry me but how can he when he's disfellowshipped? It's not fair! Why is he being so stupid and selfish?"

"I'm in the room," Caleb said softly. "Of course Arthur can ask me. I do think you're too young to marry, but that's a different topic."

"Don't listen to him," Madge said. "I married at your age."

"And look how that turned out," Caleb said.

Madge focused on Ciara. "Any problems in our marriage aren't to do with me. If your father just kept Jehovah at the centre of his life, and stayed committed to The Truth, then you wouldn't be in this situation."

"Who's going to walk me down the aisle?" Ciara cried. "It's Dad's job. It's his spiritual responsibility! He knows he can't do it if he's disfellowshipped!"

Neither Ciara nor Madge made eye contact with Caleb or included him directly in their conversation.

"Mum, make him repent. Make Dad go to the elders and apologise. Make him come back to us."

"I'm only going to say this once," Caleb said kindly but with conviction. "You have a choice. I have a choice. I've made mine. It's up to you what you do. Of course I want to walk you down the aisle and see your wedding with Arthur. He's a lovely lad. But do I do that to the cost of my mental health?"

"Yes!" Ciara stormed out of the small blue-walled kitchen, and raced upstairs. "I hate you, Dad. I hate you. You're so selfish!"

Before leaving the kitchen, Caleb turned to Madge. "I refuse to keep living like this. I feel so out of place in my own home, and that's not right. If you and Ciara continue to shun me, even within the privacy of our home, I will leave. That's a promise, Madge. I take our vows seriously, but I'm not prepared to be bullied into believing and acting in ways that aren't who I am. I'm not the person you married."

Bearing Gifts

It was a picture-perfect Autumnal afternoon, the way the world comes alive with vibrant coppers, mustard and gold. It has a way of fooling you, and the colour gives no clue as to the losses and solemnity of the Winter days which will soon follow.

Grace was packing up soaps for her distributors. Just three hours till she needed to pick Lilac up from school. As the clock ticked, Grace wondered if she'd manage to get every task done.

While moving a box nearer to the door of the conservatory, to make it easier for when the courier came to collect them, Grace noticed a car coming up the lane. It wasn't a vehicle she recognised and immediately felt herself on edge. The past couple of years had changed her. No longer completely carefree, but always that bit wary in case her past came looking for her, Grace made a policy of not having visitors unless by prior arrangement. Surely not Jehovah's Witnesses again? She dismissed the thought. Maybe someone is lost?

When the car stopped and the driver got out, Grace gasped. No. No, it can't be!

Was this really happening? In an instant, Grace knew that there was no way she'd get her orders out with the courier today. It would be an impossibility.

Washing her hands at the sink, with her favourite cleansing soap, Grace quickly wiped them dry and then ran out the door.

"Oh my God, I am at the right place!" a voice called to her across the garden. "I never thought I'd find you!"

"Angie. Oh Angie. I can't believe you're here. Why didn't you tell me you were coming to England? I'd have met you at the airport. Come here!" she called, and they embraced in a way that only best friends can do. "I have missed you so much. You'll never know what an ache this has been. How long are you here for?" Grace barely gave Angie room to move. "Come inside. Come! We'll get your bags later. Tell me everything."

Grace settled Angie in with a pot of tea, and they caught up with each other's lives. Although they'd messaged each other almost every day since Grace left Australia, there was no comparison to the joy they both felt sitting in each other's presence. Friends since kindergarten, there wasn't anything they didn't know about each other.

They settled into the sun-bleached floral-print cotton sofa in the conservatory for a while, and then Grace continued packing her orders for the courier to collect, while they reminisced about happier times in life.

Inevitably, the topic of that fateful day finally reared its catastrophic head, yearning to be made visible.

"I still haven't told Lilac what happened. I don't know if I ever can. She asks about Mum every single day, and when she'll see her again. I'm so scared she'll hate me forever. Mum and Lilac were thick as thieves, you know? Best friends."

"Grace, you can't hide it from her forever, and I suspect that the longer you leave it the harder it will be for both of you. It's not my place to say, though. I'm not her mother. You have to do what you feel is right. I can't wait to see her. I bet she's so tall now!"

They chatted for some time, ate raspberry and white chocolate muffins, and belly laughed their way through old stories. Once the courier had collected the boxes, Grace said "Let's walk to school and meet Lilac."

That afternoon, when Lilac came skipping out of her classroom, it was all Grace could do not to cry with joy. There was a happiness to her daughter that was growing stronger with each passing day, despite the loneliness she'd often expressed from being apart from her grandmother and former friends. It took Lilac a few moments to reconcile Angie's familiar face in front of her. They'd had countless video calls over the past couple of years, but to see her standing outside the school gate confused her.

Angie had been in Lilac's life since the day she was born, and had been a constant presence.

Angie scooped Lilac into her arms, then wiped tears from her eyes as she said "You're so tall! Look at you! Every bit as beautiful as you ever were. Oh my goodness you're gorgeous!"

"Angie, did you bring my grandmother? Did she fly over on the plane with you? Where is she? When can I see her?"

Neither Grace nor Angie anticipated those questions, certainly not at the outset of their reunion.

Grace looked on helplessly as Angie took charge. It was a path that had to be walked gently, but Grace herself didn't know how to begin.

"Let's talk about that later when we get to yours, shall we? I want to hear all about your school. It's so lovely. I want to play on those swings myself and sit on the wooden unicorn. I bet you have so much fun here!"

Grace watched as Angie, a preschool teacher, did what she did best: bring joy, fun, excitement and the gentle caress of kindness and care. Angie and Lilac were several metres ahead of her on the walk home, as they skipped by copper beech trees and listened to a woodpecker.

"Shhh. Look," Lilac whispered, pointing to something in the grasses. "It's a dragonfly. Mummy says they mean angels are nearby."

The blue insect darted in the warmth and stillness of the September sunshine. All three of them studied the creature, active in the shoals of light patterning upon the stalks of grass. It was just metres away from the water's edge of a nearby pond.

Grace reflected on the evolution of dragonflies, going back two to three hundred million years, and with that very thought her life's problems disappeared into insignificance amongst the shadows.

That evening after Lilac was tucked in bed drifting off to sleep, Angie unpacked her bags ready for her two-week visit.

"I've brought you something," she said. "I wasn't entirely sure I'd get it through customs because of the botanicals, but here you go. Thought you might like these."

Grace unwrapped the package, instantly aware of the contents long before she saw them. The scents were of home and of *mother*.

For some time, she simply held the soaps in her hands, breathing them in, shedding tears of joy and immense sadness.

"This is so thoughtful, Angie. Whatever made you think to bring these?"

"You left me with enough soap to last twenty

lifetimes. It just seemed obvious to bring some here. Soaps that your Mum made. I knew how much it would mean to you."

"God, I miss her. Most days I swear I can hear her when I'm soapmaking or cooking soup or out gathering plants. It's like she's right there beside me, and then she's not. It's hard to describe. It's not her voice, as such, just a feeling. A presence."

"I can't bring her back for you Grace, but maybe breathing in the soap will help to feel like she's closer again?"

Mother Song

It was a breezy yet sunny morning when Angie offered to walk Lilac to school and give Grace some time on her own.

Grace wrote her to-do list, mindful of carrying on with work commitments while making the most of this unexpected visit from her best friend. Angie would be leaving in five days, and though she wanted to enjoy every second with her, there were also orders which needed fulfilling.

Grace looked at her mother's soaps on the kitchen bench, untouched since the day Angie gave them to her, torn between using them and allowing the scents to fill the kitchen, or leaving them in her bedroom drawers as a keepsake. If only the soap could cleanse her soul, soothe away the sins of the past. Grace held a bar of freesia-and-vanilla soap in her hands, and breathed in the scent.

"Hello love," came Serena's voice, clear as day. "I'm still here. I'm still with you. I love you. Please stop feeling guilty. None of it was your fault. None of it. It was my time."

"Mum? Mum? Is that you? Is that really you?"

"Yes, love, it's me. I'm always here, you know? Right beside you. Talk to me anytime, just like you always have."

"Why haven't I heard you before? Why can I only hear you while touching the soap you made?"

"Maybe you wouldn't have believed it was me otherwise. But with this, you know."

"My heart aches for you. I feel so lost. I try hard to make a wonderful life for Lilac, but it just isn't the same without you. She asks for you all the time. How can I tell her what happened? The truth will erode her trust in me."

"The truth will set you free, sweetheart."

Their conversation continued until she heard Angie open the door. Grace placed the soap on the windowsill, and a sense of peace descended on her.

Frozen

It was the tenth morning in a row that Madge hadn't spoken to Caleb in any way, not even perfunctory instructions. He'd tried not to count, but after the third day it was hard not to notice how long she was carrying on her vow of silence. Even though he was disfellowshipped, there was no need for her, Chell or Ciara to oust him from the fundamentals of family life. Perhaps she had other reasons for punishing him, and this served as the perfect cloak. The only requirement for her, as a Jehovah's Witness, was that in the home they didn't share in spiritual teachings. Caleb glanced at the clock. In two hours he was meeting Grace to talk through the renovation of her old barn. Thrilled at seeing her again, he was also grateful that there'd finally be an influx of income. For reasons he couldn't understand, they'd been financially haemorrhaging for some time now. Night after night he'd twisted and turned through nightmares of being homeless on the streets of Carlisle, begging passers-by for a mouthful of food or small change to buy a coffee.

"This can't go on," Caleb said to Madge when she walked into the kitchen that morning. "I know you're not happy with my decision, but there are consequences to your behaviour too. If you want me to say here, providing for you, your Mum and Ciara, then please accord me the respect I deserve if not as your husband then as a human being. And if you want me to leave, if you want a divorce, then tell me. Tell me now. I know that when we married neither of us could have foreseen that I'd change and not want to be a Witness anymore. But I have! I want freedom. I *need* freedom to think for myself. If you can't allow me that, then what choice do I have? Do you really think I want to walk away from my family?"

Madge picked up her handbag, and without even a cursory glance, headed out the door.

Caleb slowly walked up the stairs, and into the bathroom. One thing he'd learned in recent months was just what a difference a hot shower made. Somehow it let everything wash away. As he waited for the water to heat up, he grabbed a new soap from his toiletry bag: Sunflower and Saffron infused with the scent of yellow freesia.

It occurred to Caleb that their essence of Summer was far at odds with the snowflakes drifting outside the window. He thought about Grace's words: *sunflowers symbolise following the God of your understanding.* She'd explained how it is considered a spiritual flower because it reminds us of the Sun, and our search for light.

Saffron is for affluence, luxury and wealth, she told him, then added her other reason for including a single strand of saffron was that it enhanced the potency of her invocations, and amplified the way she charged the energy and the protection it offered.

The soap was infused with the scent of yellow freesias: *for friendship,* she said. Caleb was deep in thought reflecting on their friendship, and how easily they'd confided in each other about the stories of their lives, their hopes and vulnerabilities. How different this friendship had been from all the others he'd experienced in his life, where their commonality was faith in Jehovah. With Grace, it seemed as if their bond was their faith in each other. This was an experience unlike anything he'd ever had before.

Caleb smiled and acknowledged that he'd only chosen the soap this morning for its bright colour and *not* for the intention Grace had set. Would she be disappointed to know that? As he washed, the tiny suds formed a gentle foam. He watched as they bubbled between the black hairs on his arms. Somehow, with each caress of the soap, he could think more clearly as he washed away the harshness of Madge's stubborn silence and Ciara's daily dramatic discussions with her mother.

"Show me the way," he whispered into the stream of the shower spray. "Jehovah, show me the way. Please." Caleb breathed in the scent of the soap, wondering what gave it such an addictive smell. Just freesia? What else did she add? Perhaps he'd ask Grace later. "Surely, Jehovah, I can love you without having to conform to idiotic man-made rules? Show me. I beg you. I don't know who I am anymore! My family is falling apart. Everything I've ever known is disintegrating. If I stay, it will destroy my soul. If I go, it will destroy my family. What do I do? Please show me the way!"

It was no longer possible to hold the angst and anger of recent months within. The rush of water down the drain invited him to let go, let go, let go. *Come with us*, said the suds as they whirled away. *Come on. You want a life of riches unlike you've ever known before? Then get out of the shower, get dressed, and choose the life you really want. Only you can do that.*

Caleb placed the soap on the holder, alongside three other pieces of soap he'd been using recently.

Madge's soaps, the one from Grace, and her bar of Palmolive unscented, sat in the far corner of the bathtub.

Anger cracked open the vaulted door of Caleb's heart, and layer upon layer of silent sadness swept its way through his body in waves of grief.

Mourn, if you must, then move on.

Who said that? The voice was as distinct as if there was a person in the bathroom. Caleb concluded that it was of his own imagining, something emerging amongst the onrush of tears.

For another twenty minutes, he stayed within the sanctuary of solitude that the shower afforded him. At some point before he left the house this morning, he'd no doubt see Ciara and Chell. The last thing he needed was any obvious sign he'd been crying. No doubt Ciara would mock him and then accuse him of betraying the family and Jehovah.

For some time after the shower, Caleb stood in front of the mirror, shaving, and studying the shape of his face. *Who am I?* When he thought of Grace, he could identify exactly who she was. An ordinary woman to others, perhaps, but to him she was a woman who made magic through honouring incantations she'd learned at her grandmother's side, and ones she created through her own learnings and observations. He wondered about the soaps she formulated and if they were really the source of the secret spells or if they came from deep within Grace. Where did the qualities emanate from? He shook his head. *Am I going mad?* Before he met Grace, he'd never given a single thought to soap. Ever. It was a constant and reliable thing in his life, for sure, but a scentless bar in the shower with one purpose only: to clean. These days he couldn't stop thinking about soap.

Were the soaps from Dragonfly Cottage even made for cleaning?

Sunflower and Saffron Soap,
infused with the scent of yellow freesias

It was the height of Summer when she gathered our petals. She'd grown us especially for this task, but not all of us would necessarily be used. That decision was ours, she said the day she planted us in the ground. Back then, we were tough black seeds, the fruit of our mother sunflower, encoded with everything we'd need to grow to our majestic height, bloom to capacity, and reach towards the light. Like all our radiant mothers before us, we hold the stories of turning towards the Sun.

Joy. Our purpose is joy. To bask in the radiance of Divine Light, and simply be our bright, beautiful and bold selves. We were born to be seen, to rise above, and flower in majesty.

Just 15mm long, and about 4mm across, we were drop-shaped seeds: our fragile kernel embraced within the safe cocoon of our hard black-and-white-striped shell.

Each seed was held, and she whispered a story to us about helping those souls who needed guiding towards their own God.

Help them find the light.

And with tenderness, she slipped us into the cool earth, covered us over with a blanket of dark soil, and let us find our own way. Our Maker had no need to lift the soil and see if we were sprouting. She trusted that growth comes out of the dark. Within a few weeks, we heard her exclamations of joy as we first peered above the ground, tender green shoots waving "Hello. We're here!"

We sensed her motherly instinct to protect us from the ravages of howling winds, heavy rains and ravenous rabbits! We were tiny, to be sure, but with time we grew leaves, and then, at last, what she'd been waiting for: a bud. Within about three months we'd transformed from a seed to a fully blossoming flower.

Dozens of dazzling golden crowns adorned the edge of her country garden, looking longingly to the Source of life.

That day, the day she gathered our petals, she saved our babies.

Some for seeding the next year's flowers.

Some for nourishing her and her baby.

Some for the mother-and-baby feathered friends who visit her garden.

Many petals were dried slowly in the sunshine, and others were infused into oil; all preserved until the day we would be added to the soap. And then we heard her words as she stirred us into the vat:

Whoever holds this soap,
Know that you are a source of light
Your God is within you.

See the light.
Reach for the light.
Be the light.

May happiness and good fortune shine upon you.
May it be all around you.
May it radiate from deep within you.
Blessed be.

And that's when I came along: a single strand of saffron, the colour of sunrise. Considered the world's most expensive spice, my beauty and purpose come at a high price. I am the essence of affluence and wealth. Your historians have noted that, at times, I have been worth three times the price of your gold.

Ours is a mystical power guiding the bearer to the secrets of the Universe.

I am from the stigma of the *Crocus sativus*, coming to bloom in the Autumn. I'm little more than a fine thread, with a yellow tendril at one end, and at the other, a flute. There are only three of us for each flower, and therefore to produce just one ounce of us takes thousands of flowers. Gold, indeed. Magic, if you will.

Before coming to my Maker, I grew in the fields of Kashmir, the saffron capital of India, dancing alongside meadows of purple crocus flowers. In gentle breezes, we were surrounded by towering snow-capped mountains. When the time was right, local families gathered us in wicker baskets. Our flowers are tiny, and this job is not easy. My flower, and all those beside me, have three parts: petal, yellow strand, red thread. The purest of saffron is from the red strands, and we are dried over a charcoal fire. Harvest time means festival time, and saffron farmers offer us at the shrine of *Hazrat Sheikh Sharif-ud-Din*. So significant are we, that our stories appear in songs and poems with those of the sufi saints who brought us here.

When our Maker added me to the soap, it was with respect for my ancestry, and place on Mother Earth. She knew I was a long way from home, and said it was not a decision she made lightly. My holiness, she said, was vital for imbuing the recipient of the soap. As she opened the glass jar in which we'd travelled across the seven seas, she breathed in our aroma: sweet, earthy, somewhere between the gentle Summer smell of alfalfa and the sweet lusciousness of raw wildflower honey. Our Maker said that, although she didn't grow me in the garden, our connection was decided long ago. She kept a strand inside her purse, wrapped in a small piece of muslin, to invoke blessings of the Goddess of Wealth: Mahalaxmi. And then our work began.

Protect this person
Bless them with riches
Show them abundance in every moment.
Let their days be guided by gratitude.
And so it is.

And then I was carefully placed along with the sunflower petals. We rested deep within the creamy rich batter, enveloped by the scent of yellow freesias. Although I was a long way from home, I don't suppose I've ever felt more at home in my life. This was what I was born for: a thread of gold.

We were told that the freesia scent wasn't just an adornment but symbolises friendship, and the ability to show grace no matter what pressures may be present in life. It was a beautiful day, breathing in the sensual salient elixir so sweetly scented of citrus, Summer rain and strawberries. We were ready, the three of us. We'd come together, at long last, and in friendship we rested in respect and reverence for six weeks until she was ready to send us on our way.

Conversion

Just before Caleb stepped through Grace's front door that morning, he flicked the snowflakes off his coat. How much longer would this cold snap last? As he looked back at the snowflakes falling behind him, he wondered if he should perhaps head straight back home. There was no telling how long it would be until Grace's no-through road became impassable. Perhaps he should have phoned and rescheduled? When Grace opened the door, they both held back from their instinct to hug. Somehow it was as if they'd always been in each other's lives, and yet on other days there were all the tentative steps of a new friendship: *Do you like this? Do you like that? Why? Why not? Here, try this.*

"I don't think I'll ever get used to this weather," Grace said, inviting him in out of the cold. "Give me a hot Summer's day any day of the year!"

Caleb loved her ability to be so natural, welcoming and friendly, even on a day that, by its nature, had her out of her natural comfort zone.

"Come through," she said, even though he knew her house inside out. "Let's have a cuppa before we go to the barn, shall we?"

"Sounds good. Thank you."

Conversation with Grace was easy, as ever. There were no sharp edges to her, at least none that he'd ever noticed, even when she was being direct or they were talking about uncomfortable topics. It was her way of simply being herself, genuine, interested and caring, that had him letting go of fears, confusion and doubt, bit by bit. After he ate her third homemade blueberry-and-coconut muesli bar, Caleb laughed "You better show me the barn before I eat you out of house and home!"

The three-hundred-year-old stone building was at the far end of the garden. And although he and Lilac had hit a tennis ball against the outside of the barn wall many times, he'd never been inside.

Grace opened the double wooden doors. "These could do with replacing for a start," she said, wincing at the splinter now embedded into her thumb. Unsuccessfully, she tried to wheedle the slither of wood out with her teeth.

"No problem. I can do that. I'll make a list of all the jobs you want doing, and then we can prioritise them."

"Mostly, I need as many curing racks as we can fit in here, and storage cupboards to keep rodents out of my supplies.

Caleb walked around the perimeter of the spacious barn, tapping at edges, bending down here and there and peering into nooks and crannies. It occurred to him that the barn was bigger than his whole house.

"Well, one thing is for sure, Grace. This barn has great bones. It's strong, secure. Really, it just needs some TLC. What's your budget? Once I know that, I can be realistic about what we can and can't do."

"There's no budget."

Taken aback, Caleb said "You have to have a budget. I can't be clear about wood, materials, style, time and all the rest if I don't have a budget to work to."

"Caleb, there's no budget. I have…"

"Ballpark figure, then?" has asked, trying a different approach.

"I have resources I can tap into, Caleb. There's disposable income from a property I sold in Australia. I want to invest it in this business, and in this barn. You're right. It does have good bones. I feel that so strongly. I can't imagine not ever working in the studio—I love the light-filled conservatory—but my business is expanding in ways I didn't foresee, and I need all the space I can get. But I don't just want a shed, you know."

"You want a beautiful space?"

"Got it in one! You're a quick study, Caleb," she laughed.

"Ok. So, no ballpark?"

"No. Just create. Make magic for me!"

"I'll leave all the magic to you, Grace," he smiled. "Right, I'll share my initial thoughts. I'll write them up for you to ponder. To start with, it could benefit from four to five skylights to let in more natural light. Maybe even six. Even though it will primarily serve as a storage area, in the long run it will save on electricity costs if you can come in here during the day and not have to switch lights on."

"Yes, of course."

"This arch-shaped double door could be made wooden, a replica of what is currently there, or it could be double-glazed with wooden frames. Again, allowing more light, but also as a feature. And can you imagine how much this barn would benefit from the view of those meadows and fells? What do you think?"

"Sounds beautiful! Not just a storage space, but a beautiful additional working area."

"The curing racks I can almost do in my sleep now," he said, a smile accentuating his dimples. "If it were my building..." he stopped, hesitating.

"What? If it were your building, Caleb? What would you do?"

"I'd invest in solid wooden flooring. I don't know what you had planned, but this concrete can easily be overlayed. The wood would add warmth, beauty, and be a lot easier to walk on. So, practical and pretty."

"Absolutely."

"You're really sure about the no-budget thing, aren't you?"

"100% sure."

"The storage units can be completely functional as built-in cupboards or could be a mix of that and stand-alone feature pine dressers. It's really up to you. Perhaps the first thing to focus on is the floor and closing up any holes or rodent entry points, and installing the skylights. That way, you've immediately got an additional storage space."

"Caleb, you really do make all this seem so easy. Thank you!"

When she threw her arms around him in delight, it was all he could do not to breathe her in: the subtle scent of jasmine rising from the warm nape of her neck. *God help me*, he said to himself as the hug lasted longer than he expected. *Does she have any idea what she does to me?*

If he ever needed a cold shower, it was now. Without soap! Especially her soap!

"Thank you," she repeated as she stood back.

"My pleasure, Grace. When would you like me to start?" he asked, avoiding eye contact for a moment and surveying the barn.

"Now! Right now!" she said impatiently, and then laughing. "Whenever you can. Obviously I'll fit in with your work schedule. But whatever and whenever you can convert this barn, it will change my life. Well, my working life at least!"

"I dare say it will change my life, too," he said, with that all-to-familiar half smile.

"How do you mean?" she asked.

"Nothing. Never mind. I'm grateful for the work, Grace. Thank you for trusting me with this project. It's huge, and I appreciate it."

"Caleb, talk to me. What do you mean it will change *your* life?" she asked, dragging a dusty haybale from the corner for him to sit on.

"The more I spend time with you, the more clearly I can see my life, my former life, for what it was and, well, still is to some degree. The distance helps me. I've spent my life trying to recruit people, you know? Saying 'Would you like to study the Bible with us?' Although our teachings are very much based on Armageddon coming at any moment, and that divine forces will kill any non-Jehovah's Witness, I always held onto the promise of a New World. A bit like converting this barn, I suppose. I'm looking at the end point: the promise. The whole teaching, to my mind anyway, is based on this idea of 'just around the corner'. The fear we've been indoctrinated with, though, is psychologically disabling. We're always warned about the dangers of worldy life, and staying well away from it, and away from non-believers. And yet, when I come here, when I'm with you and with sweet little Lilac, I…" he stopped, the old guilt of apostate rearing its ugly head.

"You feel free of that?"

"Yes, mostly."

"Caleb, every human on this planet should be free to live life, and experiment and explore new things. It's only natural to cultivate friendships, to be curious, to celebrate, and to experience peace. There is absolutely nothing wrong with asking questions. I will fully support you in reclaiming your birthright. Trust in the magic that comes with new beginnings. You can do that."

"And my family? Do I just turn my back on them?"

"I don't understand."

"I had to choose between my family and freedom. The faith stops members leaving with dignity and integrity. There is public shaming designed to bring you back to your senses. Since I've been disfellowshipped, my family has barely spoken to me. My friends no longer have anything to do with me. My whole community, gone, just like that. It's everything I've ever known. Most of my work which comes from brothers and sisters in my community has dried up. So many of them cancelled their work with me. So, yes, this barn project is changing my life, both in terms of work and income, but more than that; it's about being treated kindly by another human being."

What Caleb wasn't expecting was Grace's reaction. She sat down beside him on the haybale, and placed her hand on his.

"When something is familiar, Caleb, there is comfort to be found there. It can make it feel right even when it isn't. That's why so many people stay in abusive relationships."

"I'd been easing myself away for a while, you know, skipping meetings and the door-to-door ministry. But when you're disfellowshipped, everything changes. It's like you're dog crap on someone's shoe; and they'll do everything they can to get rid of you so they aren't associated with you. It's the worst feeling in the world. There's a level of humiliation that's forced upon you. I can't even begin to explain it. I feel lost, Grace. So lost," he said, finding comfort as her hand gently squeezed his in acknowledgement.

"Have you ever had counselling?"

"The Watchtower magazine counsels against it. 'The devil will destroy your faith if you enter into therapy', so they claim. This is what we're indoctrinated with our whole lives."

"We're designed to heal, Caleb. No matter what we've been through in this life, we can heal. I do believe that."

"I'd like to believe that. My whole life has been fashioned by the beliefs of others. I feel so angry and cheated. The harsh reality is that I have few marketable skills. The teachings hold a taboo against college and university. Not only did I have my higher-education aspirations restricted, but also my leanings for sport, and even my passion for politics. And as for celebrating things like birthdays or Christmas, well…"

"So they've made you totally dependent on them for your identity?"

"Yeah."

"I can see that more clearly now. I don't have the answers for you, Caleb, but this I do know: the more you unplug from the doctrine, then the more you can tilt towards your curiosity and let it lead you elsewhere. We're not much different from plants, you know? People need to grow too. We need the right conditions in which to thrive. It's all very well for me to say that you should let go of the past and focus on the present, but I'm not in your shoes. All I can offer is this: free yourself from all the threats and warnings, and follow your own heart."

"Is that what you did, Grace? Is that what brought you to this ice-cold country?" he asked, shivering in the unheated barn.

"In a sense, yes. I chose freedom. Psychological freedom." She stood up, and started moving towards the door. "Have a think about counselling, Caleb. Might make a difference. It helped me, to some degree anyway."

Caleb wondered if she was deliberately bringing the conversation to an end now that the focus was on her. There was a definite shift in the temperature.

"Shall I install a woodstove in here too," he asked, catching up with her.

Disappearing Mother

For three weeks, Chell barely left the bed. Caleb and Madge's bed. The bed he'd crafted as a wedding present for Madge. With each passing day, Madge could see her mother slipping away. A solemnity settled over their small two-bedroomed cottage, and made way for the inevitable smell of death.

"Maybe it's time for the hospice," Caleb said gently one morning. When Madge didn't reply, he added "Or Hospice at Home? We could have a bed set up here, in the living room. What do you think? Madge, will you please answer me? How can I help if you keep refusing to talk to me?"

Madge turned to look at him, and for the first time in months spoke directly to Caleb. It was like talking to a stranger; a person she'd never met before, and yet her stomach twisted in knots lurching this way and that: this was the only man she'd ever made love with; the father of her child, and a man who'd been consistently kind and considerate across the years even when her own behaviour was lacking in goodness.

At breaking point, she snapped: "My mother is dying! You want to fix that? You can't! But if you want to help me then come back to the Kingdom Hall and repent. It's that simple, Caleb. Just do it! Keep this family together."

"Madge," he said softly, but it was all she could do to refrain from slapping him. Why did he always have to be so nice!

"If only you came back to Jehovah, then everything would be better. When Mum dies, I need you at my side. I need you, Caleb! Be the responsible husband that you promised to be. The spiritual head of this house! Come back to Jehovah. Come back to me. Please. Please do this for me."

"And me? What about what I need?" he asked, gently shrugging his shoulders in despair. "I've spent our whole marriage putting you first. You know that, Madge."

"Stop making this about you! Don't be so selfish."

"I'm going to call Hospice at Home, and make arrangements for Chell's care. I can't be here to help care for her and earn us an income."

Madge sat on the sofa beside Caleb, gently weeping for the mother who was disappearing from her life.

"I never thought she'd grow old and die," she cried. "The New World was going to be here and Mum would be part of it."

"I know," Caleb whispered, gently placing his arm around her shoulder. "So did I. We all do. After all, the New World is always just around the corner. It's a hard thing to come to terms with. We've spent our lives believing that."

"But it *is* just around the corner!" Madge shouted. "It is! And I just need Mum to live a bit longer so she makes it. Otherwise…"

"Otherwise?" he asked.

"When she's dead, that's it. There's no body, no soul. Nothing. How can my mother just become nothing? I don't understand!"

"Nor do I, Madge. Nor do I."

"My world is falling apart, Caleb. Ciara will be leaving home when she marries Arthur. Mum will be gone. You're always out working. I feel like an empty shell!"

"And Jehovah? Have you turned to Jehovah?"

"Of course I have. Every moment of every day!"

"And?"

"There is comfort from studying his teachings, and being with others. But I want my mother to stay!"

"Of course you do," Caleb said, holding her hand, the same hand he once held when he made vows and placed a ring on her finger.

"Is there anything I can say that will bring you back to Jehovah?" Madge asked, wiping a tear from the corner of her eye. "Anything at all?"

"What makes you think I ever left Jehovah?"

Day of the Departed

The afternoon light was dim, held back by furious pewter-coloured clouds, as Caleb drove Madge, Ciara and Arthur into the parking lot at Carlisle Crematorium. Immediately he could see so many of his beloved brothers and sisters getting out of their cars. These were his people, his community; friends he'd known his whole life long, and yet he also knew when he stepped out of the car not a single one of them would make eye contact or talk to him. Even today. Not even on the day they came to say goodbye to Chell.

That was their duty, their spiritual responsibility: *to shun Caleb from their lives until he came back to his senses, into the fold, and returned to Jehovah.*

Although he could feel his shoulders shift into a soulless sinking, and that familiar sense of not being good enough, Caleb refused to be caught in the manipulation. Abruptly, he adjusted his posture and his tie, and stood tall. Today was about remembering his mother-in-law, a simple but kindly lady who'd never been a spot of bother in his life.

As they waited under the covered area of the blandly designed 1950s brick building, Caleb never strayed from Madge's side. He might not be welcomed into the congregation, but today he was a husband, son-in-law and father, and there wasn't anyone who could deny him that as much as they might try.

Madge was grieving for her mother.

Ciara no longer had her maternal grandmother.

As he continued to be excluded from condolences and conversations, his mind wandered back to Grace.

Perhaps it was the lovely maintained gardens around the building that brought her to mind. Even in the depths of Winter, there was a beauty to be found here. And beauty was something he instantly associated with Grace. Just the other day, she'd given him a bar of Cypress and Violet soap for Madge. He'd placed it in the shower, but not said a word. This morning, he'd noticed it had been used but whether that was Madge or Ciara he couldn't be sure. The balsamic, woody smoky lemon scent lingered in the steam long after their shower.

When the funeral director led the procession, and made his way up the driveway, followed closely by the hearse, a hush came over the crowd.

How could he support Madge and Ciara at this time, when his own mortality was in question? What happens when we die? Is that *it*? Is everything that ever gave us our life force just gone? Not only our body, but our soul too? Was everlasting life a myth? So many questions, and no one to answer them.

When Caleb reached for Madge's hand, she pulled away. In her hour of need, it seemed she didn't need him after all. Or was she keeping up appearances? He couldn't decide.

The mourners followed the coffin into the chapel, and an elder led the service.

Is this it? Caleb thought to himself. *We live our whole lives and then at the end, just a few words to sum up our story? What was the point of any of it? Why were we even on this Earth?*

Twenty minutes after they'd processed into the chapel, it was all over. As the recessional music played, one by one the congregation dispersed as mourners followed Madge out of the chapel and along the length of the flower-filled hallway, the scent of roses and carnations clinging to the warm air and guiding their way.

Caleb observed how readily the community held Madge, and did so with a kindness and care that was withheld from him in equal measure. Finally, after a few minutes of total exclusion, a member came up to Caleb and said "It's best that you don't come to the funeral tea. It wouldn't be appropriate."

"Chell was my mother-in-law!" Caleb said, keeping his frustration to a hushed tone.

"Please, Caleb. It's not my decision. The elders asked me to relay the message. Please stay away. For everyone's sake. Someone will bring Madge and Ciara home."

As Caleb separated from the crowd, and headed back to his car, he felt yet another piece of himself die.

Cypress and Violet

When our Maker first held me in her hands, she bowed her head in reverence and stood in silence. *Graveyard Cypress*, she whispered after a while. She already knew of us, as is her way, and listened to our stories as we spoke of far-off lands rich with fables and folklore.

Many of our kind flank the edges of old cemeteries: guardians of the threshold, and keepers of secrets and stories. Our ancestors in Greece and Rome were collectively known as 'the mournful tree'. Many of them were planted by graves, or in front of homes. Branches often lay at the base of graves prior to interment. Our boughs hung outside of houses to signify a death had taken place, and others used us in funerary rituals because our delicate fragrance can mask the smell of death. But we, we the cypress, are so much more that that. And our Maker knew this. Yes, we're associated with death and mourning but to be in our very presence is to surrender into your sorrow, and that is when we stimulate the sanctity of healing. Our job is to help overcome the lamenting and loss of bereavement. To be clear, it isn't to rush or hurry the process. It has its own time and rhyme, season and story. We are merely enablers so the energy doesn't become trapped.

It was our association with the eternal life of the soul, she said, that she most wanted to bring into her soapmaking: a sense of hope. *For tears to flow*, asking that we comfort and console.

You may know me as Violet, and some call me Heart's Ease. You might be attracted to my pretty colour, and yet my sole role — indeed, my soul role — is to mend your broken heart. I do this by bringing you peace, calming your nerves, and instilling the truth of tranquillity.

Our Maker matched us with cypress to bring a balm to the broken. We are here to serve. Tiny we may be, but never underestimate our power to enhance protection spells and accompany your visions and dreams. Our heart-shaped leaves are like blades. It would be foolhardy to dismiss us wildflowers as nothing more than weeds just because we grow in abundance in pastures, riverbanks, hedged areas, open woods, and cliff ledges.

Our Maker gathered us one fine Spring morning, baskets of us, and preserved our petals by infusing us into sweet almond oil. This would keep us whole, she promised, until she was ready to call upon our services. When the time was right, she also included some purple Brazilian clay into the soapmaking process to bring a richer colour to the soap.

The Day the Lilac Bloomed
26th September, six years earlier

Serena and Rebecca began their day early, packing a picnic lunch before heading off for a walk around Wategos Beach near Byron Bay.

With Rebecca's baby due any day, they were mindful not to stray too far from home. For two hours, they enjoyed a gentle stroll along the track which meandered through the rainforest. Eventually they trekked over the cliff tops and stopped for a while to take in the views of the hinterland and ocean; a sense of spaciousness surrounding them.

"I'm ready for lunch now," Rebecca laughed even though she knew it was barely ten am. "I'm always so hungry!"

They found their way onto the sheltered little beach, and Serena spread out their picnic blanket and lunch. For a while, they sat in silence and watched the gradual break of the incoming waves as they spread out over the ample sand bar. It was one of their favourite places to visit whenever they closed up the soap shop and had a day out. A family-friendly beach, it was the ideal spot for children to swim in the salty water and play in the sand. Under the watchful eye of Cape Byron Lighthouse, they ate and chatted.

"I wonder if the baby will arrive on time," Rebecca said, watching a toddler run by her to escape having its nappy changed.

"They arrive when the time is right, and not when everybody else thinks they should. Just take one day at a time, my love, and don't keep looking at the calendar. Listen to your body, Rebecca. Make friends with it. It's the best home you'll ever live in."

"And my baby's first home. I hope my baby is happy in there."

"I have no doubt about it," Serena said, taking her daughter's hand into hers. "She couldn't have chosen a better mother."

"She?"

"We both know she's a girl! We only do girls in this family," Serena smiled.

"Even though I declined all the scans they offered, I've always been sure this baby is a girl. I don't know why."

"Mother's intuition."

"Did you know I'd be a girl?" Rebecca asked, looking into her mother's eyes.

"From the very first moment," Serena said, holding her hand.

Rebecca then napped for a while, and when she awoke she noticed her mother was out paddling in the sea water. Serena and Angie were the best friends she'd ever had, and now someone new was joining her. *Was her heart big enough to fit another person into her life?* How different would things be with the constant companionship of a baby?

When Serena returned from her paddle, she asked "Shall I take you home now?"

"Yeah, let's go."

When they arrived back at Rebecca's homestead, she stopped to smell the subtle spice scent of lilac which was coming into bloom. It was such a pleasant aroma. For two to three weeks each year it drifted on the breeze into her bedroom.

"Why have I never made a soap from lilac before?" she asked Serena.

"Probably because there are so many things we can use that it's often easy to overlook what's right in front of us."

Rebecca studied the bush for a few moments. When Serena had given her the plant as a housewarming present she warned against leaving it in a pot. "They like to spread out a lot, so be careful where you plant it. The roots don't actually grow that deep, but they love their freedom. Give it room to go where it needs to go."

"Okay," Rebecca said at the time, not giving it much further thought than that she'd like to breathe in the scent of blossom from her bedside.

"That's everything packed up and put away," Serena said, slipping her sandals back on.

"Mum, can you stay? Please. I can't describe it, but...can you stay?"

"Are you having contractions, love?"

"No, not yet. I just feel like I need you here."

"Okay, sweetheart. I'll pop the kettle on and make us tea. Chamomile?"

"Raspberry leaf, please." Rebecca felt herself consciously breathing more deeply.

"Are you sure you're not in labour?"

"I'm not having any contractions, Mum. I just feel... I don't know. It's like I want to roll up in a ball and sleep but I also want to move and, actually more than anything, I just want a cuddle," Rebecca said, wiping away a tear and leaning into her mother's long hug.

"Oh honey, I'm here. I'm not going anywhere. Listen to your body. It'll tell you what you need. Listen to her. Listen to your baby, too."

"I don't know what my body wants! It keeps

telling me something different. How do I know what to listen to?"

"Listen to your breath, Rebecca. Your breathing has changed a lot. Listen to that."

"I just want to blow out big breaths."

"Then do that."

For the next ten minutes, Rebecca paced the room, hands on hips, following the lead of her full-moon belly. "She's not due for two weeks, Mum. I'm not ready for her yet."

"Sure you are. You've been ready since the day you knew she was coming. What do you need? You've got more clothes than any baby could ever wear. The birth pool is set up in your bedroom. I've filled the freezer with meals. Everything's okay."

"But I'm not ready. What if I don't know how to love her? What if I'm not a good-enough mother? What if I'm not enough? Oh my God, Mum, she's going to rely on me for everything!"

"As is the way of every baby who has ever been born."

"Yeah, but she'll never know her father. I'll be doing the work of two parents!"

"Do you think for one second that me and Angie won't be there every step of the way? We'll always be there for you. For both of you. I promise, love."

A deep and powerful surge forced its way through the centre of Rebecca's body, calling to her "NOW!"

"I think I need the toilet. I *really* need the toilet. I need to poo. Now."

Serena beckoned Rebecca to sit on the edge of the bed. "Let me take a look."

After a few moments, she looked at Rebecca and

said "It's time to call the midwife, sweetheart. Your baby is on the way. I'll fill the birth pool but I wouldn't be surprised if this little one arrives first."

"But I'm not in pain. How can I be in labour?"

They'd already had practice runs to see how long it would take to fill. Even with the hot and cold water running, they were still looking at about half an hour.

Rebecca breathed her way through the ongoing pushing sensations which had completely taken over her body.

"I'm not ready, Mum. I'm not ready."

"Sweetie, you'll never be more ready than right now. Breathe, just keep breathing. Try not to escape the feelings in your body. Lean into them. I'm going to be quiet now, and dim the lights. Remember when Cashmere had kittens?"

"Yeah. Please don't tell me I'm having six babies!"

"What did Cashmere need from us?"

"Nothing. She just found a dark corner and wanted to be left in peace."

"Exactly. That's what you need too. The midwife will be here soon. Don't forget to drink your tea. I'll fetch some water."

"Stay, Mum. Please don't leave me. I don't know how to do this."

"You don't need to know. You need to *feel*."

"I don't know how much more I want to feel this."

"Are you in pain, my love?"

"No, it's not pain. It's just so bloody intense! I can't escape it."

"Then don't," Serena whispered.

A few moments later, she placed a cool wet facecloth on Rebecca's forehead. "Lavender," Rebecca said, breathing in the scent. "That smells so good. Thank you Mum."

"The pool is full now," Serena said. "I'll just check the temperature before you get in."

Seconds later, Rebecca slid into the warm water instantly feeling her whole body relax.

"This feels so good. This is amazing. Mum, thank you. Hiring this pool was the best birthing gift ever."

From time to time Rebecca leaned forward over the edge of the birthing pool, letting her body be held by the comfort of the water.

With each new sensation, she placed her hands between her legs and felt herself expanding. "She's coming! My baby's coming. I can feel her head!"

"You're doing great, sweetheart. Brilliant job. Well done."

"What do I do now?"

"Just keep listening to your body."

"The midwife's not here."

"You're the one giving birth, so listen to what your body wants here."

"Can you check me?"

Serena nodded, and gently shone the torch into the birthing pool. "She's coming, sweetie. Do you want to catch her or shall I?"

"You!"

"One more big breath honey."

And with that, a wet and wiggly baby slipped seamlessly from one watery world to another, and straight into her grandmother's hands. Just as Serena placed the infant into Rebecca's arms, the midwife walked into the room.

For some time, Rebecca couldn't stop crying as she cradled the infant against her chest.

"Oh my God, you're so beautiful. Hello, Lilac. I'm going to love you so much. More than anyone has ever loved another person before. You'll always be safe with me. I promise."

Building the Future

It was the gentle rhythm of each day that Grace and Caleb grew to love. In the morning, not long after Grace had taken Lilac to school, Caleb would pull into her driveway, unpack his tools, and head over to the barn. Grace would meet him there with a coffee and scone, and they'd sit in comfortable silence for a few minutes before she headed to the studio.

One of the first things she insisted happen, was the installation of a log burner so he could work in warmth and comfort. Grace had also brought in a radio so he could listen to music, too. She noted he straddled between jazz and classical, and on cloudy days it was rock 'n' roll from the 1950s. More than once she found him dancing along. Even though they spent most of the day in separate buildings, just knowing he was nearby made all the difference. By late morning, she'd bring him another drink and tell him to pop over to the kitchen for lunch not long after that.

"This floor is amazing!" she said, when Caleb finally placed the last few pieces of solid oak lengths down. "Good enough for a ballerina. Really, Caleb. It's brilliant. Thank you so much."

"I'll rub it down with beeswax, if you want to go down the eco-friendly route rather than varnish. Just be prepared to do it every year or so. It's a big job. A huge commitment."

Moonlight Sonata was playing on the classical music station, and as they made eye contact Grace forced herself to stand back. What she really wanted to do was hug him, not just to thank him for the magnificent carpentry work but because he filled her days with a comfort and solidity that had long been missing from her life. One day, but not today, she'd tell him. Somehow she'd find her voice and let him know that he'd changed her life.

"I'm glad you agreed to it. Everything else will be like icing. This floor gives a solid base. It really will make all the difference for you."

"I can see that already. It's just perfect. Look, I've made some beetroot and walnut burgers for our lunch. Come on over in about ten minutes?"

When Grace returned to the kitchen, she finished prepping the lunch then went to the sink to wash her hands. Ever since Angie had visited, Grace kept Serena's soap in the kitchen.

"You were right about everything, Mum. I think Caleb might just be okay, you know? As for Lilac, I still need to tell her about you."

"Who are you talking to?" Caleb asked when he walked into the kitchen.

"Mum. I'm talking to my Mum." Grace hung up the hand towel, and said "Ready to eat?"

"Your Mum?" he asked. "She's here?"

"Yes."

"I don't understand." Caleb looked into the next room, and then back in the kitchen and up the hallway. "Where is she?"

"In my heart."

"Oh. I'm not entirely sure I follow, Grace," he said, sitting at the table.

"My Mum died. Her death is the reason I'm here in England. It's a long story. I'll tell you some day. Burger?"

"Grace, tell me now. You know so much about me. You're a vault to my deepest, darkest thoughts and longings. You always seem to ask questions that have me talking far more than I ever would to anyone else. And yet, I know so very little about you. I want to know you. I want to know more. Sometimes I feel you change the subject all too often. Don't you trust me?"

The Didgeridoo

Two and a half years earlier: The Channon, Australia

The second Sunday of each month was always dedicated to holding a stall at The Channon Markets. The 'Make it, Bake it, Grow it' ethos ensured it was the most popular outdoor market in Australia. Even though the day was long, it was easy to keep Lilac entertained due to the live acoustic music and performances from local artists as they were right next to the soap stall.

Set within the panoramic view of the hinterland, locals and tourists enjoyed alfresco dining beneath the mature eucalyptus trees, which offered dappled shade from the scorching sunshine.

When the stall was set up ready for the day, and before the market opened to the public, they'd wander around to view the crafts, arts and produce on offer at some of the other 249 stalls. This satisfied Lilac's curiosity and usually resulted in purchases of some sort of recycled, repurposed or repaired wares.

Rebecca kept half an eye on her daughter while serving customers at her stall. Lilac listened intently as the didgeridoo player talked about his instrument.

"Some people say it got its name from the sound it makes when it's played."

He blew into the end of the wooden instrument to demonstrate. "In our tradition, it's played in ceremony, and when those around us are dancing or singing. There's a special way we play which is called circular breathing. As my lips vibrate, I catch quick breaths of air through my nose. It can really help someone with their breathing, such as when they have asthma," he said, playing some more to show how his lips moved.

Lilac raised her hand up high.

"Yes, you have a question?"

"I have asthma. Would a didgeridoo make it go away?"

"It has certainly helped a lot of people. There are didgeridoos of all sizes, and some made especially for young people, like yourself."

"How do you make one?" she asked.

"They're made from the trunk of a eucalyptus tree that's been hollowed out by termites."

He played some more, and the meditative drone gathered many onlookers at the market. The ambience invited even those who thought they weren't interested, and soon dozens of people, young and old, were dancing to the percussive rhythms.

"Traditionally," he said afterwards, "the didgeridoo is painted using ochres, natural earth pigments."

As the player neared the end of the performance, he said that there are some aboriginals who say that the didgeridoo has been around since the Dreamtime.

Today was just another Sunday market day, with lots of sales and chit chat with locals and tourists. What was different was Lilac's desperation for her mother to purchase a child-sized didgeridoo. She'd been enthralled by the sounds, and tried to convince Rebecca that it would cure her asthma. Rebecca wasn't so sure at first, until Lilac begged her to ask the man.

If it wasn't for the fact it had been a particularly busy day, and soap sales were double the normal flow for market Sundays, she'd probably never have bought that didgeridoo. Distracting Lilac for a while, the purchase was done surreptitiously and Rebecca agreed to pick up the didgeridoo from his shop in the morning.

The next day after driving Lilac to preschool, Rebecca opened the front doors of the soapmaking studio and turned on the air conditioning.

"Hi Mum!" she said as Serena walked through the door a few minutes later.

"Hi darling!"

They greeted each other with a long hug, and Serena began prepping soap ingredients.

"I'm just popping down to the juice bar before we open. I'll pick up some food for lunch too. I won't be long," said Rebecca.

"Okay, sweetie. See you in a bit."

Rebecca couldn't help but smile as she walked along the main street. To one side was the turquoise sea dotted with surfers catching a break, and on the other were awning-shaded cafés which already had outdoor seating filled with tourists dining on breakfasts like poached eggs and sautéed spinach, roast mushrooms, tomatoes and smashed avocado on rye.

Some shop fronts were draped in crystals, while wind chimes tinkled across the new day. Artisan gifts beckoned people indoors. As she caught sight of herself in a shop window: white shorts, lime blouse, copper hair up in a ponytail, Rebecca had to pinch herself. Life was so damn good.

Once in the music shop, she held the instrument in her hands. Rebecca had to admit the didgeridoo was pretty cute, and she could just imagine Lilac blowing the life out of it. Rebecca hoped that the sound wouldn't drive her to distraction. She tucked it under her arm, and stopped at the counter of the juice bar to order a couple of drinks.

The town clock chimed 9am, a reminder to hurry up and head back to the shop.

"Here's your juice, Mum. And look at what I bought for Lilac's birthday."

"She'll love it!" Serena said, brushing her fingers along the side of the didgeridoo. "It's beautiful. Look at that craftsmanship."

Rebecca placed it under the counter for safekeeping. Lilac rarely came to work with her so it would be out of sight until her birthday in a few weeks.

The first hour was relatively quiet for a Monday but by morning tea, the shop was crowded as locals and tourists scanned the shelves, rummaged through baskets and searched the drawers, surveying the dozens of types of soap on offer.

Rebecca was ready to decorate the wrappings of her latest batches of cured soap. Heading out to the back of the shop, she reached for a large glass jar brimming with dried purple waxy crowea blossoms. She smiled as she heard the sound of the bells chime as the front door opened. Another customer. Sure was turning out to be a good day!

"Everyone get down on the floor, now!"

Screams penetrated like glass shards into every last corner of the shop.

"Now!"

It had been years, but in an instant Rebecca knew the voice: Kev Crowman. Lilac's father.

"I said get down. Stay down!"

Gunshots exploded around the room. The stench of charcoal and sulphur from the gun smoke clawed at her throat.

Shaking, Rebecca quietly placed the glass jar down. The sound of her staccato breathing was deafening. Fumbling in her pocket, she pulled the phone out and texted her best friend, Angie: Lilac's preschool teacher.

```
Call the police! Urgent.
Kev has gun.
Keep the kids safe.
```

"Where's Becky?" Kev yelled.

Rebecca knew he was asking her mother. When Serena didn't answer, he shouted again.

"Where the hell is she? Tell me or I'll shoot you too!"

Desperately praying for the sound of a police siren, but knowing it was way too soon, in a moment of clarity Rebecca pressed the record function on her phone. She slipped it under the counter as she slowly stepped out with her hands in the air.

"I'm here, Kev. Put your gun down. Whatever it is you want, I'm sure we can figure it out."

Although she hadn't seen him since the night Lilac was conceived, he didn't look that much different. *Rough diamond*, Serena had called him. *Without the diamond. He's not good for you.* Their one-night stand had been a mistake in terms of trying to reignite their turbulent and toxic teenage years. Even at the time, she knew it was a bad idea. It was common knowledge that life hadn't been kind to him. The bitter look on his face spoke the truth.

With the gun aimed straight at Rebecca's head, she dared not lose eye contact with him.

"I want money, and a lot of it. I know your family's got loads of money. I'm taking one of you as hostage. You choose, Becky. You or your mother!"

An elderly lady, stuttering and gasping, was being rocked gently by her husband through a suffocating panic attack. They huddled together behind a table.

"Serena, get over here!"

"Leave her, Kev. You can have me! Please!"

"No, Rebecca. I'll go. Take me," Serena said, offering herself willingly.

As the old woman's panic attack escalated, Kev spun around and swiftly shot her straight through the head. "Shut the fuck up!" At the sight of her brains splattered against the wall and floor, everyone in the room stayed still barely able to breathe.

"I'll take you both, I reckon. Serena, over here I said. Sit here!" Calmly, she walked across the room. For ten years Serena had worked side by side with Rebecca, bringing magic-infused sweet-scented soaps to the heart of this popular seaside town. A unique, deeply bonded mother-daughter relationship, more like best friends, not a day passed by where they weren't in each other's company. This shop was their second home. So many memories, conversations, laughter and lattes infused their creative projects.

With his gun firmly lodged against Serena's head, he ordered Rebecca to join her.

Two teenage tourists clung to each other in the corner, sobbing. "Don't kill us. I want my Mum," one of them pleaded.

"Shut up! I can't think! Stop snivelling!"

It was impulsive, instinctive even, but in that moment as Kev was looking at the girls, Rebecca's eye caught sight of the didgeridoo and she picked it up. With every ounce of her being she lunged forward and swung it at Kev's head. Just as she brought it down, he flinched and ducked to one side. A bullet fired killing a Danish man, aged about 40. As he slumped to the floor, the full force of the didgeridoo sliced across Serena's face. She wouldn't have been aware of what happened, the coroner's report would state some months later. It was all so quick. One minute she was here, and the next second gone.

Rebecca didn't hear the sirens come from both directions of town. Nor did she see Kev bolt for freedom out the back door. And she no longer heard the screams and cries of strangers. The only thing she saw was her mother's beautiful face, which had been ruptured by Lilac's birthday present, bleeding profusely onto the shabby-chic white-painted floorboards. The floorboards they'd painted together when they first opened the shop.

"Mum, come back. Come back! Wake up! I need you. Lilac needs you." With her face buried deep in her mother's neck, she didn't hear the female police officer say "She's gone. I'm so sorry but she's gone. Rebecca, there's nothing you can do."

The shop was cordoned off, and the victims' bodies covered while police escorted the survivors outside and began the task of gently ascertaining the events which had taken place.

When Rebecca was escorted out of the shop and down to the station for further support, she asked "Lilac? My daughter? Is she ok? I need to know she's okay."

"Yes she is. Let's get you out of here, and then we'll bring your daughter to you."

Like a slow-motion movie, the ride in the police car felt like someone else's life. Rebecca noted every azalea shrub in bloom, and how the clouds were being hustled in from the east by a ruthless wind.

There was a hint of a thunderstorm in the air. As the car pulled up in front of the station, Rebecca noticed the colour of her hands. The blood of her mother's death was embedded within the life line of Rebecca's palm. She rubbed her hands vigorously against her white shorts. It made no visible difference other than leaving a layer of crimson on her clothing. She rubbed harder, furiously, and screamed "I can't get it off!"

It was with extreme gentleness that the officer guided Rebecca into the building and found a quiet, comfortable room where she could wash her hands.

A trauma counsellor was drafted in, and arrangements made for Lilac to stay with friends under discreet police surveillance.

"Have they found him?" Rebecca asked. "Have they found Kev?"

"No, not yet."

"And you're sure he can't get anywhere near my little girl?"

"You have my promise. It's Fort Knox around there. Lilac thinks she's having a sleepover tonight. She's none the wiser about what happened today."

A Place In His Arms

After Caleb listened to every last detail of that day, he held Grace in his arms for the rest of the afternoon. Words weren't necessary. Grace had said everything that needed to be said, and now there were no secrets between them. As she lay there, he thought about the many times she'd offered him words of wisdom, and acknowledged the pain that comes with being out of place. How could they have known each other all this time, sharing so much, and yet the very thing that turned her life on its axis was where she'd held herself back.

"You look wrung out," he whispered, tucking strands of hair behind her ear. "Can I get you a cup of tea? Anything?"

Grace shook her head. "No. I'm fine just here. Thank you, Caleb. Thank you for listening. For holding me."

"Thank you for sharing that with me. I don't know how you go through this world so lightly, and so lovingly. I can't even begin to imagine what you went through, and yet somehow you have made a new life for yourself. It makes my issues seems so petty and insignificant. I'm sorry for all the times I went on and on. I really am."

Grace attempted a smile. "Our stories shape and define us, don't they? One person's nightmare is another person's celebration. We can't compare. Don't lessen what you're going through by comparing it to my past. We're both out of place. We're both in exile. And I'm pretty sure we're both searching for Eden. For paradise."

"And yet…"

"Yet?"

If he didn't have the courage to say it now, he doubted he ever would. "I've never felt more at home and at peace than when I'm with you."

"I feel it too, Caleb. I really do. A different time, a different place, I suppose? Another lifetime, maybe? I need to go and get Lilac from school. Will you stay for dinner? She'd love to see you."

"Of course I will. Would you like me to stay afterwards while you tell her about your Mum?"

"I'd appreciate that, thank you."

"I wish you lived in our home, Caleb," Lilac announced matter-of-factly during dinner that evening. "You belong here," she said, pushing a carrot to the edge of her plate. "If you lived here, we could play every day. We could fly kites, you could visit me in the treehouse, I could come to the barn when you're working. And you could come with Mummy and I when we're in the fields foraging. What do you think?"

"Lilac. Enough," Grace said gently. Lilac was articulating everything she'd felt in her own heart, but he couldn't live here. Not when he had a family of his own.

"But why Mummy? Grandmother told me it was so."

"Grandmother? What do you mean?"

"When I was washing my hands with the soap."

"What soap?"

"That one? Over by the sink. She talks to me whenever I wash my hands. Grandmother agreed it would be a good idea too."

"Did she?" Grace wondered how on Earth she

could transition from this to the truth she had planned to share tonight.

"She also said not to be angry with you. That everything is okay. That she's okay. What did she mean by that? She wouldn't tell me. She said it was your job to answer that."

Grace rubbed her eyes. It had been such a long afternoon. "I tell you what. How about you eat that carrot up that you've been pretending doesn't exist, then have a bath, and I'll tell you what she meant?"

Lilac picked the carrot up with her fingers and gobbled it down.

"Can I take grandmother's soap into the bath?"

Grace hesitated; she wanted to hang onto that bar of soap for as long as possible, and certainly didn't want it disappearing down the drain.

"Please Mummy? I love it when grandmother talks to me. Pleeeeeease?"

"We have so many soaps, Lilac. You've got dozens in your room, there are hundreds in the studio. Does it have to be *that* one?"

"Yes!"

"Right. Go get your pyjamas, and I'll get the soap and run the bath."

"I'll do the dishes," Caleb said.

Later, Caleb and Grace sat on either side of Lilac on the sofa. "You sure smell good," Caleb said. "Is that scent your grandmother's soap then?"

"Yes. You know, I think that was the best bath I've ever had," Lilac said, snuggling into both of them.

"Why's that, honey?"

"Grandmother. She was laughing and reminding

me of all the things we used to do together."

"That's lovely."

"Mummy, she said you shouldn't feel sad."

"Did she?"

"She says she knows you didn't mean to hurt her. That it was an accident."

"That's true. It was an accident."

"Mummy, she told me that one day we'd be together again. She promised! But she said it was going to be a long long long long time from now: when I'm an old woman, one day I'm going to fall into a deep sleep like she did, and she's going to be there and pick me up in her arms and carry me all the way to the stars. She told me it's like the fairylights in my treehouse. Doesn't that sound like the loveliest place ever, Mummy?"

"Perfect," Grace and Caleb said at the same time.

Although she could hardly speak, Grace whispered "Your grandmother loves you so much, Lilac." Grateful for Caleb's thumb wiping the tear from her eye, she kissed Lilac on her cheek and breathed in the scent of the soap; the scent of Serena.

"I know she does, Mummy. She told me. Can Caleb sleep in our house tonight?"

"No," they said softly, in unison. Their hearts said something else altogether.

Wild Nettle and Heather

The Springtime showers brought the meadows back to life with a lusciousness that couldn't help but put a skip in Grace's step. With each passing day, her friendship with Caleb grew deeper. They'd made a home in each other's company, and it was one they treasured.

As Caleb worked, day after day, bringing the barn to the beautiful space they'd both envisioned, she also held space for him as he negotiated the changes happening in his own life. Madge and Caleb had continued sleeping in separate rooms even after Chell had passed away. Somehow the chasm seemed too huge to cross, and in his heart Caleb didn't wish to spend his night dreams alongside Madge. Grace sensed that, at some point, he'd have to choose between continuing to live in this way or do the very thing Jehovah's Witnesses don't do: divorce.

Grace reflected on how he'd need to maintain his resilience if he wanted complete freedom, and with that thought she felt the formulation of a new soap recipe emerging and jotted some notes in her journal:

Wild Nettle and Heather
Nettle: to walk through the flames of fire, and step into the primordial power of transformation. To protect. Connection with inner fire to free from a victim mindset. A reminder of power. A tonic for commitment, purpose, and resilience.

The purple heather which grew on the hillside at the edge of the land was used by a local beekeeper for his hives. She chose the plant for its signature: it often grows in places where few other plants care to set down roots, and has an ability to beautify an otherwise dreary landscape.

Grace drew on the energy of the heather to guide her in recipe creation.

Heather: confidence and independence.

There were bundles of heather branches drying in the spare bedroom. Plenty for her purposes, she decided. All she needed was to gather some fresh nettles.

After she picked up her basket, she walked through the garden towards the rusty black wrought-iron gate which led out to the meadows and to the foot of the fellside. Caleb was outside the barn measuring some wood.

"I'm just heading up the field to forage. Fancy joining me? Seems a shame to miss out on this sunshine? I won't dock it from your wages," she laughed. "Come on. You've not had a look at the rest of the property."

"Well, I have been curious!" he said.

"Let's go," she replied, and they followed the overgrown path.

"How much land do you have?" Caleb asked.

"About forty acres. Half of it is set to wildflower meadows, and the other half is fellside. One of the farmers grazes his sheep, and a beekeeper has some hives there. Most of my botanicals come from this land, but I also go up higher onto the land of a hill farmer I know."

They chatted about the lay of the land, and how much she was still learning about Cumbria, and how cold she found it: culturally, politically and climatewise.

"It's taking so much adjusting. I thought that being in an English-speaking country would make the transition okay, but I feel so far from home."

"And yet you've made a home. You and Lilac."

"It's a daily job. I don't know how I'd manage if it wasn't for my work. Being with the plants connects me. I've had to learn so much. It occupies me so that I'm not reliving trauma all the time."

They settled upon an area of richly fertile soil with a profusion of wild nettles.

"This is the best time of year to pick them. I also use them to make soup, or steam instead of using spinach, or to juice. These will be for soap. How about you hold the basket and I'll gather them?"

Caleb held the willow basket by the handle, always within easy arm's reach of Grace.

With each plant, she took a moment to listen to what they had to say:

Yes, you can gather me.
No, leave me in the sunshine.
In a little while. Come back later.

"Why didn't you pick those ones?" Caleb asked, his voice barely a whisper.

"By the time I was two, my grandmother taught me to never pick the first one you see. I should have applied that to my love life!" she said, thoughtfully. "The other thing she showed me was to always leave a gift." Grace placed a small hessian pouch.

"What's in that?" Caleb asked. "Or is that top secret?"

"Powdered sage, a tumbler of rose quartz, and a small lob of clay with wildflower seeds."

When her basket was full, they sat in the sunshine warming their skin in the rays which had felt absent for so long. After a few minutes of silence, they stood up and began walking home.

"So, what is the nettle soap for?"

"New beginnings," Grace whispered, sensing that life was about to turn.

"For you or for other people?" he asked curiously.

"For us, Caleb. For us."

As they stopped and looked in each other's eyes, neither of them resisted. Their arms wrapped around each other, like long lost friends, and then welcomed each other home to the comfort of familiarity.

"May I kiss you, Grace?" Caleb asked.

"I thought you'd never ask, but…" the words were barely out of her mouth and she didn't have time to finish her sentence.

In a life steeped in sensuality, enriched with scents, fragrances and aromas which could transport her anywhere to any place in time, Grace had never known such pleasure. Caleb held her gently, and they found a new place far away from the beauty of botanical soaps and the burden of biblical scriptures.

Fly in the Ointment

While Grace worked in the studio that afternoon, basking in the bubble of her walk with Caleb and the tender kisses they shared in the Spring sunshine, she couldn't help but smile. Could it be that the apple wood, rosemary and bay soap she'd crafted last year was finally working? *Is this what love feels like?* She'd set the intention in the soap for love, but it occurred to her that maybe she should have been clearer: was love enough? Was it ever enough? Maybe she should have added 'an uncomplicated love'. Madge was never far from her thoughts, and although Grace figured the woman hadn't helped herself at all with deliberately shunning Caleb, even though she didn't have to, she was still his wife. And then, just like that, the joy Grace had felt started to shift to discomfort. The connection between her and Caleb was undeniable but was that enough? Could it be enough? What would sustain them during the demolition of his family life? As the twist and tie of tumult inched its way through her body, slowly the memory of his kisses ebbed away.

Don't go, she whispered to the fragmented feelings of their kisses. *Stay with me.* Grace stopped the work she was doing, and decided to head over to the barn. Right now, more than ever, she needed to be with him: to feel the surety of what was blossoming. A nagging feeling was nipping at her heels, like a dog which just wouldn't let go, telling her that this was too good to be true. A woman like Grace didn't deserve love.

When she opened the barn door and saw him sawing a piece of timber, a sense of calm washed over her whole being. *You're safe,* she said to herself. *He's here. You're safe. You're together.*

"Hey," she said, sitting down beside where he was working.

"Hey," he replied, kissing her. "Are you okay?"

"Yeah, I am now. Missed you."

"Already?" he laughed.

They sat back, gathering their thoughts, and reflected on how different everything felt now. For a while, they held hands and enjoyed the silence. After a few minutes, Caleb stood up and grabbed his bottle of water from the far wall. They both turned at the sound of the old door creaking open.

"Madge?" Caleb said. "What are you doing here?"

Grace didn't know whether to be more shocked that Madge had tracked them down to this end of the garden or that she was even here in the first place.

"May I help you, Madge?" Grace asked, jumping to her feet. "Are you here to buy soap?"

"I'm here to tell my *husband* to come home."

The caustic tone to her words was all the proof Grace needed as to why she'd felt so unsettled in the studio earlier.

"Is something wrong? Is there an emergency, Madge?" he asked, alarmed by her presence.

"Come home now, Caleb," she said, then turned, calling out as she left. "Now!"

Grace raced to the door and watched Madge walk through the gardens, and around the conservatory. Once she heard the sound of her car heading down the road, she turned to Caleb.

"She might be your wife, but this is my home and I don't want her here under any circumstance. I need to feel at peace here, and that has just felt like a God Almighty earthquake."

"I'm sorry," he said, walking over to her and placing his hands around her waist. "I'm so sorry."

"So, are you going home?"

"At the end of the work day, as planned. If there was an emergency, she'd have said so."

"Caleb, it's nothing personal against her but I really don't want her to ever set foot on this property again."

"I can promise you she won't. I'll speak to her tonight. You have my word."

Grace walked away from the barn uncertain what to do next. She felt violated, and although Madge wasn't a robber or some thief in the night, she was an intruder whose energy was quickly being felt throughout the garden.

Go away from here, Grace whispered.

Leave, and never come back.

This is my home, not yours.

My family, not yours.

My life, not yours.

My love…

For the next few hours, she stayed inside the house unable to focus on anything other than vacuuming, putting away the dried washing, and cleaning the kitchen. *Breathe,* she told herself many times. *You're safe. This is your place.*

Home

When the postman dropped off the mail that day, Grace immediately spied the airmail letter from Angie.

It made her laugh that, despite modern technology and their daily messages and regular video chats, they still kept up their tradition of writing each other letters. It was something that they'd done right from kindergarten: drawing pictures. As they grew, their letters became more sophisticated. On the page they found a place to share feelings, make each other laugh, confess their crushes, and savour memories. And now, living oceans apart, it had enriched their friendship even more. Grace would often press flowers, and slip them between the pages of her letters. Angie would find exotic perfumes and spray them on the paper. There's be cartoons and they'd use coloured pens and stickers.

Grace eagerly read through the first three pages of the letter, and Angie's enthusiasm for her upcoming life plans, before slowing down.

Grace, she wrote, there's something I need to tell you. I know you don't watch the news so there's probably no way you'd find out but there's something I need to tell you. I was going to tell you on Messenger or on Facetime, but I wanted you to be in your own space to take in this news, and to think of the consequences for you and Lilac. Make sure you're sitting down.

There's no easy way to say this so I'll just be direct: Kev's body was found on a railway track. The verdict is out on whether it was suicide or just bad luck. It could be that, given he was on the run, he was trying to hide from some local police and ended up slipping as he headed down a hill towards the track. Not that I have even an ounce of pity for him (of course I don't!), but it can't have been easy being on the run for the past two and a half of years. No one knows if he had anyone helping him or where he took shelter.

At first I was in two minds about whether to even tell you. Would it bring you relief to know that you no longer need to hide? Or would knowing the truth bring up so much pain, not just about your Mum but about your relationship with him? So, I hate to be the bearer of this news, but I am here if you want to talk.

It's really got me thinking, though. Grace, you can come home now. You've got friends here, Lilac has friends. I'm sure it wouldn't take long for them to remember each other and just carry on.

And don't even start me on the weather. How can you compare that icebox of England to these sunny climes? I know you've worked really hard to build up your business there, and fantastically so. I'm in awe of your ability to rise like a Phoenix. I'd never want to take away that accomplishment from you. But as your bestie (and you know how direct I am), let me remind you that Australia is your home. I have missed you so much. I know we made a vow when you left that we'd be in touch with each other all the time, and we absolutely have, but you have to admit that heading out to the beach together, or having a cuppa on the promenade like we used to, is sooooooo much better than Facetime. So, what do you say? Obviously you can stay with me for as long as you want while you look for your own place. That's a given.

You moved to England for one reason, and one reason only: to keep you and Lilac safe from Kev. He's gone now, and can never cause you any more hurt or harm.

Come home, Grace. There's nothing to keep you in England now. But there's everything here to bring you home.

Always loving you, Angie xxx

Everything except my mother. Grace paced the studio. The news was overwhelming. Angie was right in some ways. There was no reason to stay in England now, but it would be a massive dislocation to take Lilac out of her sweet rural school; and for Grace to close down her business, only to start up again in Australia. *God, Angie. Why did you have to tell me?*

In a couple of hours, she'd need to set off to meet Lilac at the school gates. Grace listened to the quickening of her heartbeat. What choice do I make? Stay or go? What will bring us more happiness? Where do I belong? Grace felt herself shaking, and slowly let herself cry with guilt, grief, regret, and sweet relief. *Kev was gone!*

Recognising that she was finally free, though not free of the trauma, Grace headed outside to the garden. If there was ever a place she truly felt at home it was when immersed in Nature. Although Cumbria was still so unfamiliar to her, Grace had learned to look closely at the plants and terrain around her, and to befriend it as best she could.

As she walked past the aquilegia in bloom, her hand brushed the tops of them. Life in the garden taught her to keep seeing newness even in places which were familiar. Day after day she bestowed a generosity on the plant life around her by offering undivided attention. Today, however, it was hard to focus.

Stay or go?

Caleb kept coming to mind. Ever since those sweet kisses by the nettles, she'd been like a dizzy teenager. Grace knew that life wouldn't change in the blink of an eye just because of that, but hope lingered. And even today, on what ironically should have felt liberating, life was clouding over her. It would take a miracle for Caleb to walk away from the constraints of his life. Although he was the first to admit his marriage was long over, Grace figured that it would only be terminated once they were living separately and Madge was making her own way. On any other day the blackbird's tune would have lifted her spirits. Today was different, and she pondered the words she'd uttered not that long ago to Caleb: "The grass is greener where we water it."

Grace picked up the hose, and despite it having rained thoroughly for a week nonstop, she turned it on and watered the lavender. *The cycle of life,* she told herself. *And what's my cycle? Is this my ending? Is it time for a new beginning? Water the bloody garden, Grace!*

Cumbrian Moss

There never seemed the right time to bring up Kev's death to Caleb or the possibility of returning to Australia. Every time she opened her mouth to say something, instinct— or was it fear?— told her to shut up. Although there'd been at least twenty Facetime calls with Angie since the day she read the letter, Grace was still no closer to making a decision.

All morning she pottered around the studio, never quite immersing herself in any particular task. It was as if she'd lost her roots. *Moss. Moss grows without roots*, she mused.

Moss. It grows in wet places. Am I growing in Cumbria? So lost was she in her thoughts, that she didn't hear Caleb come in.

"Just checking you're okay. You usually come over by now to let me know lunch is ready. Unless you've decided to stop feeing me?" he chuckled.

Grace looked at the clock.

"Sorry. Give me a few minutes and I'll rustle something up."

"Grace? Are you okay?"

"Sure. Come and make a cuppa while I sort lunch."

"Something's distracting you. I know we've... well, we've not talked about the kiss. We need to. I want to," he said, placing his hand on her shoulder. "Are you okay?"

"Yes. I'm fine. Honestly. Just thinking about moss," she said, picking up a small piece that Lilac had left on her bench. "It symbolises new beginnings," she said, hardly finishing the sentence. "Fancy some pizza? Lilac got a bit carried away with her flour and yeast when making bases last night!"

"You're funny like that, Grace, you know, how you can go from moss to pizza in a heartbeat."

"That's me, funny Grace," she said, deflecting him once again.

"Okay, Grace," he said, "I know you well enough to sense that something isn't right. Do you regret the kiss?" Caleb asked as he flicked on the kettle in the kitchen.

"Kisses. Plural," she corrected him. "Regret? How could I regret those?"

"Then what is it? Have I done or said something to upset you?"

"No. No Caleb. Not at all."

"Are you worried about Lilac?"

"Sit down, Caleb. There's something I want to tell you."

"I knew it. I knew something wasn't right. You're worrying me now, Grace. Are you ill?"

"Sit!" she said, trying to ease her nerves.

"Kev, Lilac's father. Biological father. He's dead. And well, this changes everything for us. I no longer have to hide. I don't have to live in fear. But it primarily means that I can go back to Australia. That me and Lilac can go home."

She studied his face as he took in the realisation of what that meant, and his crestfallen look was almost too much to bear.

"You're *leaving*?" he asked, not quite taking in the news.

"Well, it's a choice. A possibility. There was only one reason I came to England, and now that reason is gone. There's a way of life in Australia that just can't be recreated here no matter how hard I try."

"And there's nothing to keep you here? *No one* to keep you here?"

"Do you want this pizza reheated or are you happy with it cold?" she asked.

"Grace, stay. Please stay. Stay for us."

"Caleb," she said, shaking her head. "How can there be an us when you're still married to Madge, and living under the same roof?"

"Grace, you know that Madge and I are long over, and that I'm just trying to keep a roof over our heads until Ciara and Arthur marry and she has her own home. I'm sorry it's complicated, but please don't rush into this decision. I know that I've brought nothing but my baggage to you, and for this I am so sorry. You deserve so much more. But, I do believe we can create a new beginning together. Be patient with me. I have to find my way, just like you did by coming here. Nothing happens in an instant."

As his heartfelt words settled in the air, they were a balm in the noisy confusion of her own mind.

When she placed cold pizza on the table in front of them, she heard the signature symbolism of the moss: *change is coming.* And then an image of Lilac giving her a bouquet of dandelion clocks came to mind.

Dandelion, she mused. *Dandelion seeds to symbolise being carried far away from where they started.*

Remembering Rebecca
Growing with Grace

From the day Rebecca became a mother, she'd risen early each morning to take some time walking outside barefoot. It was a simple practice which sustained her through the many months of disrupted sleep, breastfeeding long, long into the night, and balancing soapmaking with soothing a teething toddler. Even after her move to England, with its vastly different climate, she kept up this daily devotional to her wellbeing. Oftentimes, it was just a ten-minute foray amongst the flowers and foliage while she settled herself into the day.

On this unseasonably cool day, even though it might have seemed preferable to wrap her feet in woolly socks and stay indoors by the Aga, there was comfort to be found in the familiar: barefooted on the grass, she breathed in the soft light of day, and gave thanks for the life she was creating for her and Lilac.

Dragonfly Cottage had been a delight to create as their home. The first few months here had been spent on decorating and going to auctions and bidding on furniture. In time, it started to feel like a place they could call home. The previous owner had employed a gardener to keep on top of things, and Grace soon learned that filling in the borders with perennials and flowering shrubs rather than wall-to-wall annuals cut the gardening chores in half. There was as much joy to be found in an almost self-maintaining garden as there was in the dizzying delights of one that required constant work.

I'm still me, she mused then heard her mother say

"The garden looks beautiful, Rebecca."

These days she no longer corrected Serena when she heard her old name.

"I remember when you used to play under the macadamia trees, dancing like a ballerina."

"I'm so far from home, Mum," Grace answered. "So far."

"Rebecca, home is within. You take it with you wherever you go. This cottage, this garden, they aren't your home. They're a mirror of what's within you."

"But I feel so different here in Cumbria than I did in Byron Bay."

"That's because you aren't the same person. You can't go through what you did and still see the same world on the outside. If you'd stayed there, everything would have looked different."

"You think so?"

"I know so. You're exactly where you're meant to be, Grace."

"Rebecca. Why didn't you call me Rebecca? You always call me Rebecca!"

"Who are you? Rebecca or Grace? Who do you want to be? Do you want to remember Rebecca or do you want to grow with Grace?"

"Mum, I'm *your* Rebecca. When I remember Rebecca that's what brings you closer to me. Grace is someone you didn't know."

"And yet you've brought me here, haven't you? Can't I live in your present and your future as well as your past? Whatever name you go by, you're still you. You'll always be my daughter. My beautiful, kind, loving daughter. Nothing and no one will change that. And our relationship, well, that will live long after we've both left this Earthly life behind."

Grace sat on the bottom step of the stairs to Lilac's treehouse wiping tears from her cheeks. Ever since she started using her mother's handmade soap each day, the communication channel between them had opened completely.

"You have such strong roots, sweet child. No matter where you move to, no matter how many transplants happen, you know what to do to make yourself feel secure against the winds of change."

"You gave me those roots, Mum. Thank you."

Crossing the Threshold

"You can sleep in the house, Caleb. The spare room is exactly that. It's free for others to sleep in. There's no reason to stay in the barn."

"Honestly. Grace, the barn is more than adequate. It's just until I can find a place of my own. It's only fair to Madge that she stays in the house."

"Lilac and I really don't mind. And besides, given you work in this barn every day surely it would be nicer to sleep in the house?"

"Trust me, sleeping on this air mattress is going to be luxurious after all those months of camping out on the sofa."

"Well, if you change your mind, Caleb, you don't even have to ask. If you need anything, it's yours. You know where everything is. Help yourself. It'll be nice having you around. Make yourself at home. I mean that."

"I know you do, Grace. I know. You've been incredibly kind. I don't want to be any more of a burden than I already am."

"Burden? I'm the reason you ended up being disfellowshipped and all the problems that came because of that. The least I can do is put a roof over your head."

"It's not your fault. None of it is. Thank you, though."

"What can I do to make it a bit cosier in here for you? Would you like a wardrobe or chest of drawers or something?"

"Grace, I'm fine with things just the way they are. I do have a favour, though."

"Sure. Anything. What is it?"

"Ciara's wedding is being livestreamed tomorrow. Would you mind if I watch it on your laptop? Mine is at the repair shop."

"Of course. I still don't understand why you can't go to your own daughter's wedding. This whole thing is bloody ridiculous!"

"She's following scripture. From her perspective, their perspective, I haven't remained in the teachings of Christ. They teach that they mustn't share in spiritual or social fellowship with the disfellowshipped."

"Do you know how insane this is?" Grace said, fuming as she walked away. "Insane!"

"Grace, come here. Being angry isn't going to help anyone, least of all me. They stand firm that what they're doing will benefit me. That somehow my heart will be touched by their lack of response and that I'll 'come to my senses'. That I'll return to Jehovah. I'm absolutely devastated that I can't walk Ciara down the aisle and be there when she marries Arthur, but I made a choice. And so has she."

"I'll leave you to it, Caleb. Sorry for being angry. I just don't understand. I don't understand how they can tear a family apart like this. It's wrong. It's cruel."

"You and I can't change it, Grace. It's beyond us."

As the livestream began, Caleb wiped a tear from the corner of his eye. His baby girl was now a young woman. To his mind, still far too young to marry but he knew it was the way with Jehovah's Witnesses. It had once been his way. The constant monitoring of a chaperone led most young people to marry far too early in a desperate attempt to loosen the shackles of community control so they could finally have sex.

Ciara, the little blonde-haired girl he held in his arms and rocked to sleep for months on end while Madge lived in the mire of post-natal depression.

Ciara, the grizzly girl who seemed to teethe constantly from birth to two.

Ciara, the happy girl who sang to Beatles songs with him on the way to school each day.

Ciara, the charming girl who had him wrapped around her little finger for years on end.

Ciara, the rebellious teenage girl who seemed to forget her Dad when she spied Arthur across the congregation.

Ciara, the once faithful little friend who no longer adored her father in the way she had.

And now, today, elegant in a white wedding gown looking prettier than he'd ever seen her. Clutching a bouquet, she stepped towards the bridal car. He could sense her nervousness, and how she forced a weak smile to the elder who'd be walking her down the aisle. Madge was hovering nearby, alongside six bridesmaids, holding court almost as if it were her own wedding day.

Caleb thought back to that fateful day. Whatever possessed him to marry Madge, he'd never know. So many friends had warned him against the choice.

"She's not right for you," they said in various ways. Caleb knew that to be true, too, but somehow the wedding fever which swept through the community had him and Madge married before he knew it. How different would life have been if he'd not been a baptised Jehovah's Witness? And what path would his life have taken had he been allowed to pursue his dream of veterinary science?

What if? What if? What if?

The car arrived at the Kingdom Hall, and Ciara stepped out. Bridesmaids gathered around and ensured her wedding train was splayed around her evenly before she began the procession.

Madge beamed as if she were the Queen herself.

"What a vision of beauty," Grace said, admiring Ciara. "She really looks lovely. Can't believe how much she looks like you; that jawline and smile. Those dimples."

"I should have been there," Caleb said, a tear slipping from his eye.

Grace held his hand. "I know. I'm so sorry," she said.

"It was just too high a price to pay, Grace. To be there, I'd have had to betray myself. Was I wrong? Should I have just gone along with what they wanted? Will she ever forgive me?"

"Caleb, I can't answer that for you. You were being true to yourself, and that's important."

"I just wonder if Ciara and I will ever come back from this."

"She chose this too. Remember that."

"Did she, though? She didn't ask for me to be disfellowshipped."

"Ciara *chose* to marry at the Kingdom Hall and follow those rules. She could have got married anywhere."

"Jehovah will always come first, not her father."

They sat in silence for the next little while as the elder talked scripture.

Once the ceremony was over, Caleb sighed and switched off the laptop.

"Thank you for watching this with me, Grace. I

might just head out for a little walk. I'll see you in a bit?"

"Of course. Why don't you go up the back meadow?"

That evening as Caleb and Grace made a lasagne together, Lilac kept dancing around the dining table. "I'm so happy, Caleb. How long will you stay in the barn? Can you stay forever? Can this always be your home?"

"Lots of questions, Lilac," he laughed, patting her head. "Maybe we should just take one day at a time. How would that be?"

"Caleb?" Lilac's face was intent. "Could you be my Daddy?"

Grace dropped her knife on the floor. "Lilac!"

"It's okay, Grace." Caleb bent down on his knees, and gently placed his hands on Lilac's shoulders. "If I could choose for anyone in this world to be my daughter, I'd choose you. We're great pals, aren't we? That's never going to change."

"Yeah, but I've never had a Daddy. All the kids in my class have daddies but I don't. Never. Never ever had one to call my own. And a Daddy is someone who reads stories and plays games and makes you laugh and cuddles you when you're sad and makes you hot chocolate. And Caleb, you do all those things. So please tell me why you can't be my Daddy."

"Lilac, where is all this coming from?" Grace asked, exasperated. "Why now? Why today?"

Acutely aware of just how difficult the day had been for Caleb, Lilac's timing couldn't have been worse. The one thing Grace knew about Lilac was that once she set her mind on something she didn't stop till she got what she wanted. It had made parenting utterly exhausting, at times, and at other times Grace smiled that her daughter was so feisty and determined. Tonight was *not* one of those times.

"Right, young lady, enough of all this. Stop. Now. Please set the table for dinner. And when you've placed the cutlery, pop out the linen napkins."

"You're being bossy, Mummy! I bet Caleb wouldn't be bossy if he was my Daddy. If you stopped being bossy and listened to me, then we could just be a happy family."

"Aren't we already a happy family?" Caleb asked Lilac. "Don't we already do all the things families do together? We share meals, and go for walks. We watch movies and read books."

"Yeah, but I want to *call* you my Daddy. So all my friends know."

"If it's okay with your Mummy, it's okay with me," Caleb said, hoping to defuse the situation before it escalated any further.

"She's finally asleep," said Grace, yawning as she came into the living room later that evening. "That little rascal. I can't believe she put you on the spot like that."

"I'm sorry," Caleb offered. "I could see she was on a roll, and I thought it might nip it in the bud."

"She does see you as a father. I know that. Right from the day she met you I noticed how longingly she looked at you and up to you. And you've been nothing but kindness to her. It's no wonder she wants to put you up on such a pedestal. I'm just concerned about her attachment to you when everything is so up in the air."

"About you and I, or about you moving back to Australia?"

Starting Again

The first thing Madge did the day Caleb moved out, with just a couple of suitcases in the back of his pick-up truck, was to remove all of *that woman's* soaps from the bathroom. Madge was surprised how satisfying it was to put them all, eight in total now, into the bin. For a few moments, she stood there, seething with anger.

Soap. Soap was the enemy! And then she remembered: a long-buried memory rose to the surface begging for attention. It was the day she called a girl in the congregation a 'pig'. The memory was suddenly as clear as if it had just happened. Her father had heard, and grabbed five-year-old Madge by the arm. Without letting go, he pulled her all the way to the restroom where he washed her mouth with soap.

"Don't you ever speak like that again! If you do, I'll wash your mouth until it's clean. Do you understand, Madge?"

Sobs escaped her mouth, now. Other repressed memories haunted her, holding her in their hands and squeezing the truth from her, and reminding Madge that only 'clean' words and thoughts were acceptable. For a time, Madge stood at the kitchen window sniffing into a tissue. Once she'd regained her composure, she continued pottering about and making the house her own.

The scents of Grace's soaps lingered, though, and seemed to chase her all around the house. Eventually, she put the bin outside. And still, the scents lingered. Madge sprayed air freshener in every room, then opened all the windows and doors.

Every item that had been part of their marriage was removed, one by one. Each picture on the wall, every cushion, every darn last thing. When she opened the bottom of a dresser, she pulled out two wedding albums. Without even a cursory look inside, she took them out to the garden and put them in the incinerator with all the photos from their courtship and holidays. *Every last one.* With a single match, she set fire to her past. Today was a new beginning, and she was determined to make the house her own. Now that Ciara had moved into a city flat with Arthur, Madge had no one to please but herself and that suited her just fine.

Once she felt satisfied that everything that remotely reminded her of Caleb was gone, she started unpacking various items she'd been collecting over the past few months. Things she'd hidden in the back of the wardrobe and with her neighbour.

For some time, Caleb had begged her to stop spending so much money on new clothes for Ciara, clueless that Madge was saving it for this moment.

It had dawned on her when things first started changing in their marriage that at some point she might have to get a job. The thought terrified her. If there was anything she had to give Caleb credit for it was that he was a good, solid and consistent provider. What would it be like to provide for herself now? For months, she'd been squirrelling money away, safely putting it into a different bank account secure in the knowledge that she'd have some sort of cushion.

This afternoon brothers from the Kingdom Hall would be bringing her new furniture, including a bed. The last thing she wanted to sleep on was the marital bed Caleb had crafted for them. Bit by bit she had dismantled it and then added the wood to the incinerator. She'd remove every trace of Caleb from her life if it was the last thing she ever did. There was no way she'd ever forgive him for the humiliation he'd put her through. Never. Being married to an elder was something she was proud of as it gave her a certain status in their community. Being married to a disgraced and disfellowshipped person was unforgivable.

As she walked from room to room, letting go of a marriage and family life, Madge could see herself portrayed throughout the house. No longer were there walls in the bedroom where Ciara has scribbled with crayon as a child or Caleb's work boots under the stairs or his cafetiere on the coffee bench. She always preferred instant coffee. Quicker, she said.

One by one she hung up new pictures, and added trinkets and ornaments that spoke of the new identity she was creating. Her home would reflect this.

The one thing she was really looking forward to was having Bible-study classes in her home again. It was something they did regularly in their early married life, but increasingly over the years Caleb resisted, saying that their small home was busy enough without adding other people to it. She wondered, for a moment, if that new member to the congregation might be one of the people to come over. He'd taken rather a shine to Madge, and she was surprised how quickly she blushed in his presence.

Tomorrow she'd be starting her new job in a care home. All at once the idea of going out into the world, meeting new people, and earning an income of her own, was exhilarating and terrifying.

The phone's shrill tone startled Madge.

"Hello?"

"Mum?" came Ciara's trembling voice down the phone line.

"Ciara, what's wrong?"

Through the sobs Ciara said "Me and Arthur have had a fight. I want to come home. Please Mum?"

"What did you fight about?"

"I want him to spend more time with me but he's always out with his mates. I thought marriage would be different. And now we're fighting all the time but the flat is so small there's nowhere to go. I need space. Mum, I'm not sure I even want to be married anymore."

"I thought you loved Arthur?"

Ciara cried some more.

"I do. I think I do. I'm just so upset. Can I please come and stay with you? For one night? I miss home. I miss my old bedroom. Please, Mum?" she begged.

"No, Ciara. Where did you ever get the idea that marriage was easy? You can't run away every time you have a tiff."

"It wasn't a little tiff. We said awful things to each other and yelled and screamed. I don't want to stay here anymore."

"If you're old enough to get married then you're old enough to deal with the reality of it. I'll see you at the Kingdom Hall on Sunday. I need to go now."

Madge had always been a perfunctory sort of mother: Ciara was clean, well dressed, never missed a meal. To the outside world Madge was a wonderful mother. Where she excelled in keeping a tidy house she lacked in affection and warmth.

A knock on the door alerted her to the arrival of the brothers. Excitement had her rushing to let them in.

"Hi Madge, we've brought your furniture," Jed said. "Are you ready for us to bring it in?"

Another Chapter

"What would you think about moving back to Australia, Lilac?" Grace asked casually that morning while a pancake sizzled in the wide pan. "I'm not sure how much you remember about it, but if you wanted to go back, we could."

"Will Daddy be coming with us?", Lilac asked, with all the seriousness of someone leading a board meeting.

"Caleb?"

"Daddy. Don't call him Caleb. Well, Mummy, will he be coming with us if we go back?"

"No," Caleb said softly, entering the kitchen in the middle of their conversation.

"Then I don't want to go. Can I have maple syrup with my pancakes, Mummy?"

"Even though Aunty Angie lives there, and all your old friends?" Grace asked, just to be sure.

Caleb unscrewed the lid of the maple syrup bottle.

"If you want to go back there, Lilac, we could Facetime all the time like you do with Angie," Caleb offered.

"Nope. This is our home. This is where I want to stay. With both of you. Angie can come and visit us."

They ate pancakes in silence, and then Lilac announced she was going out to the treehouse to make soap spells.

"If you really want to move to Australia, Grace, I can't stop you. Just because the reason you came here has been removed that doesn't mean you have to go back. Surely you must have a reason to stay here?

After all, you were the one who told me that the grass is greener where you water it. Can you focus on what is in front of you?"

"Caleb, I do have reasons. I have made a life here. And I…"

"And?" he asked, sensing her hesitation to acknowledge that their friendship was finding a new path.

"And I have found *love*. I know you feel it as strongly as I do, and Lilac has it bursting out of her too."

"But? Am I not enough for you? Is it all my baggage? I understand if that's the reason. I'd be terrified of me too!" he said, lowering his head.

"It's not you I'm fearful of. My track record when it comes to relationships hasn't exactly been something that I'm proud of."

"That's only because you're defining it in one way, Grace. Look at your relationship with Lilac. And Angie. And the women at the school gates you talk about so fondly. Or the courier who comes to the door and chats to you longer than the time he has allocated per drop off, and the postie who stops for a cup of tea in the garden with you. What about the suppliers you laugh with on the phone? And then there's the way you connect with those who join you on the Extinction Rebellion rallies. They're all relationships, too."

"Well, when you put it that way."

"I can stay in the barn, for now, or move somewhere else, but what I don't want Grace, is to walk away from you. From us. Not now. Not ever. What we've got is something precious. Why would we turn our backs on that because of what's happened in the past?"

"There are so many unknowns, Caleb. I have a little girl to think of, to protect, and each day she spends with you I can see her fall more in love with the man she now calls Daddy."

"And that's why you want to go back to Australia? To protect her?"

"To give her the option. She didn't ask to move here."

"You moved here to protect her. And you've done that. You're still doing that. It's time to think about what you need now. What you...desire?"

"I know what I desire, Caleb, and what I want, but...well, there are no guarantees, are there?"

"There never have been. Not for anyone. Everything in life is a risk. Grace, I once heard you tell Lilac that it's in the midst of change that we often discover the wings we never had. You were both looking at a dragonfly hovering near the pond."

"You heard that?" she asked.

Caleb laughed. "I don't miss much between you two. You also told me to trust the magic of beginnings. No matter what sort of day you've had, Grace, I want to be your favourite place to go."

Grace reached for his hand. "A new chapter then? For both of us?"

"Maybe this is a whole new book?" he said.

"An entire life after happily ever after?" she smiled, before kissing him on the lips.

The Sweetness of Staying

Where there's life, there's soap. When our Maker crafts us, she is clear about one thing: it's not our role to take away a person's will or manipulate them in any way. No. Our job is simple: we create *possibilities*. We open doors. It's then their choice if they listen to the whispers of Destiny. We don't have a plan for whomever is blessed with our presence, but we do have a path. It's always up to the bearer what they do. Life is a choice.

Every step of the journey of Our Maker's family rested on days of sweet simplicity. They are learning that today's truth isn't necessarily tomorrow's truth. That happily ever afters are just the beginning, and that the New World isn't 'just around the corner', but right here, right now, if only we open our eyes and see.

~ The End ~

Acknowledgements

I am so grateful, once again, to the wonderfully talented artist, Sarah Esau, for creating another gorgeous cover for me. I am so blessed. Thank you.

Lynda Cook Sawyer, a beautiful friend and talented soapmaker, for your guidance and patience in answering my many soapmaking questions.

Special thanks to Jili and James from *Jili Allen Creative*, here in Cumbria, for being the brilliant dream team behind my brand designs and websites.

My darling friend, Dawn, it is such a joy to be in your company, especially when we share our love of all things botanical.

For my husband, Paul: thank you for your never-ending support of my creative life.

I am so grateful to those lovely beings in my *Author Veronika Sophia Robinson Beta Reader Community* for your support as beta readers and reviewing the Advanced Reader copies. Thank you!

Last but by no means least, I am indebted to my friends who are former Jehovah's Witnesses, for your insights and sharing real-life experiences with me. I applaud you for your bravery, honesty, curiosity, and for empowering yourselves by curating rich and beautiful new lives of freedom. *Fly high!*

About the Author

Veronika Sophia Robinson is a multi-genre indie author. *The Soapmaker* began as a creative project while studying for her Master's Degree in Creative Writing at the University of Cumbria in 2020. The module was: *Experiencing Place*. The idea for *The Soapmaker* came from breathing in the exquisite scent of handmade lavender and geranium soap; her sense of smell was keenly activated before she wrote a single word.

Without doubt, her strongest sense is that of smell. Her favourite scents include: jasmine, eucalyptus, petrichor (the earth when it rains), freshly cut grass, mango, passionfruit, the skin and hair of her daughters when they were born, lemon zest, ginger, lemongrass, coffee, lavender, lilac, cardamom, nutmeg, cinnamon, rose, mint, Nag Champa incense.

Along with being clairaudient, Veronika also has the gift of clairsalience: a psychic sense that allows deceased loved ones, and others in the spirit world, to communicate through the sense of smell.

Having lived in six countries within the span of six years, and as a new mother (with daughters born just 22 months apart) living in three countries within just seven months, her experience of place, and being out of place, readily informs her writing practice. An Australian transplant, she lives in rural Cumbria, England.

When she's not writing or working as a celebrant and celebrant trainer, Veronika can be found reading, walking in the woods or across fields, listening to music, plant-based cooking, soaking up sunshine, seeking adventures here and there, or walking barefoot in the garden.

About the Artist

Sarah Louise Esau is first and foremost a mother to two home-educated teens. She's married to Sean, who she met in Coogee Bay in Australia, whilst they were both traveling many years ago.

Sarah has over 20 years experience of working with young people both in mainstream and alternative settings. She's a passionate advocate for consent-based, self-directed education and has published many articles about education, the more recent ones you can find on her blog: www.unschoolsketchbook.com

Sarah loves to be outdoors walking with her dog, Legend, and observing the changing seasons. She's been a volunteer for mcsuk since 2016, and likes to import the wonder she experiences when immersed in nature into her drawings.

Sarah has always loved to draw and finds a deep sense of peace when sketching at home with a backdrop of music playing and a cat purring nearby. You can view her illustrations on Instagram: @slesau_art

Moonlight and Motif

Moonlight & Motif, an imprint of Starflower Press, publishes novels in the genre of magical feminism, a subgenre of magical realism. Magical feminism is based in the real, rational world, with spirituality or magical elements which disrupt our version of reality and encourage us to revision life. The protagonist, as a female 'magic maker', is symbolic of a woman who stands up to the male-dominated world. It is often a critique of patriarchy, religion, society and culture. Look out for Veronika's upcoming novels in this genre.

moonlight & motif
Magical Realism

Starflower
press

Ingram Content Group UK Ltd.
Milton Keynes UK
UKHW021054020723
424368UK00012B/200

9 781739 335397